CROW

SOULLESS KINGS MC: MARBLE FALLS, TX
BOOK 1

ANDI RHODES

BLUE JOURNEY PUBLISHING

Copyright © 2024 by Andi Rhodes

All rights reserved.

No part of this book may be reproduced in any form or by any electronic or mechanical means, including information storage and retrieval systems, without written permission from the author, except for the use of brief quotations in a book review.

This is a work of fiction and the product of the author's imagination. All names, characters, businesses, places, events and incidents are used in a fictitious manner, unless otherwise noted. Any resemblance to actual persons, living or deceased, or actual events is purely coincidental.

Cover Artwork - © Dez Purington at Pretty in Ink Creations

Editing - Darcie Fisher at Into the Gray Author Services

A NOTE FROM THE AUTHOR:

For the longest time, I thought Soulless Kings MC would end with Royal. That prospect turned patched member always felt like he was going to be the last story told. Little did I know, it would be virtually impossible to say goodbye to the SKMC world.

That being said, welcome to Marble Falls, Texas! If you read Forever Savage, my book in the Mayhem Makers world, you've already met some of these bikers. If you haven't read Forever Savage, don't panic... you didn't miss anything that will impact your enjoyment of this new series.

Some things will feel familiar, like the Nightmare Room, and others will be brand spankin' new. So, grab a bottle of Jack, kick back in your favorite reading spot, and enjoy Crow and Addison's story.

Much love,
   Andi

To all the Soulless Kings MC fans out there… welcome back!

Crow...

Growing up in Marble Falls was the very definition of boring. Fortunately, my father was the president of the Soulless Kings MC and when he met his maker, I took over the reins. Now I get to make my own fun.

But my way of life is threatened when a sexy siren walks into my club under false pretenses. She thinks she's clever, but I'm not about to let her take down my family. Holding her hostage might not be the best idea, but it's my only option if I want her to see that the Soulless Kings aren't all bad.

What I don't count on is the intense urge to keep her and make her mine.

Addison...

As the daughter of the Chief of Police, I've always strived to be the son he never had. I want nothing more than to follow in his footsteps, but he doesn't think a woman can handle the job. And I'm going to prove him wrong.

But as the saying goes, the road to Hell is paved with good intentions, and my desire to show my father what I'm made of lands me in a heap of trouble.

When I'm forced to remain at the Soulless Kings' clubhouse, I regret the decisions that led me there in the first place.

At least, until I realize that the very people I vowed to take down are the only ones who make me feel like I belong.

PROLOGUE
ADDISON

I'M GOING TO PROVE TO HIM THAT A WOMAN CAN DO ANY FUCKING THING A MAN CAN DO.

Nine years old...

"You're going to school."

I stomp my foot and ball my hands into fists at my side. It's take your daughter to work day, and my dad is refusing to take me with him. I'm going to be the only little girl in my class if I can't get him to change his mind.

"But Daddy, I have to go," I plead. "Mona's dad is taking her, and so is Carrie's. All my friends will be gone today."

"Mona's father is a dentist, and Carrie's is a mailman," he says with exasperation. "There's no chance that they could get hurt."

"You're not being fair!"

"I've made up my mind, Addison," he snaps. "Now, go get your bookbag so you don't miss the bus."

Tears spring to my eyes, but I blink them away. Daddy doesn't like it when I cry. Rather than risk him seeing my hurt, I whirl around and run upstairs to my room, slamming the door behind me.

I don't waste too much time on my feelings because it won't do me any good. When Daddy makes up his mind about something, there's no changing it. Not even his little girl can do that.

When I open my door to head back downstairs, shouting reaches my ears. Mommy and Daddy are fighting again… about me. Once I reach the bottom of the steps, I stay close to the wall and eavesdrop.

"I've made up my mind, Sharon," Daddy barks. "Addison is going to school, and that's final."

"This is a rite of passage for a daughter," Mommy cries. "Please, Jack, don't make her miss out on it."

"The police station is no place for a little girl," he snaps.

"So, if Addi were a boy, you'd take her?"

Please don't say yes. Please don't sa—

"Of course, I would," Daddy replies, and my

heart sinks. "What better way to turn a boy into a man?"

I wish I were a boy.

Thirteen years old...

"What's taking you so long?"

I stare at my panties and blink back tears. Crying isn't going to make the blood disappear. It isn't going to fix this.

"Go ahead without me," I tell Mona. "Tell Mrs. Cooper that I'm going to the nurse's office."

"Addi, what's going on?" Mona asks. "Are you okay?"

No! I'm bleeding from my naughty parts.

"I'm fine," I insist. "Seriously, go. I don't want you to get in trouble."

Mona sighs. "Call me later?"

"I will after I finish my homework."

Because that's the rule. No friends, no television, no anything until my homework is complete.

Sometimes it really sucks being the daughter of the Chief of Police.

"Okay. Talk to you later."

Her sneakers slap against the ugly bathroom tile, and the moment I hear the door close behind her, I reach for my backpack and pull out my cell.

Mom will know what to do.

But Mom doesn't answer. I leave her a panicked voicemail, begging her to come pull me out of school.

Breathe, Addison. It's just your period, not the end of the world.

Unfortunately, I'm not prepared. Sure, Mom had that talk with me, and everything I need is at home, but I never actually put the pads in my bag.

Think, Addison, think.

I could go to the nurse's office like I told Mona, but I've seen the phonebooks Ms. Hunt hands out to girls. No way will her *supplies* work.

There's only one option left.

Dad.

After entering his cell number, I hit the green call button and press the phone to my ear.

"This better be an emergency," he grumbles when he answers. "Blood or fire, Addison. Those are the only two things whi—"

"I got my period," I blurt, and heat blazes across my cheeks.

"*That* is *not* an emergency," he snaps.

"It's blood, isn't it?" I sass.

"Don't get an attitude with me, Addison."

"I'm sorry," I mutter with a sigh. "I tried to call Mom, but she didn't pick up. I need you to go home, get me some pads out of the bathroom, and bring them to me."

"Can't you ask one of your friends or the nurse for… something?"

Yeah, I could. But I don't want to.

"Please, Dad," I beg.

He clears his throat. "Where are you right now? Aren't you supposed to be in Algebra?"

"I'm in the bathroom," I shriek. "And I can't come out of the stall."

"Addison, get creative," he orders, much like he does with the officers beneath him. "I can't leave right now for something so ridiculous."

With that, he disconnects the call. Angrily, I stuff my phone back into my bag and yank on the zipper to close that pocket. I return my focus to my panties and try to figure out how I'm going to deal with this.

Addison, get creative.

Dad's words tumble around in my mind until creativity strikes. I glance from the problem to the toilet paper. Then I wrap toilet paper around my hand in an effort to make my own version of a sanitary napkin.

I really, really wish I were a boy.

Twenty-two years old...

"Next, we have Addison McGill."

Applause from the small audience fills the air as I stride toward my father. Graduating from the police academy is a big deal, but the look on Dad's face doesn't convey the excitement buzzing through my system.

I did it. I not only survived the academy, but I excelled. My marksmanship scores are the highest in the class, as are every other score for skills we were tested on.

"Congratulations, Addison," Dad says as he shakes my hand.

There's zero emotion in his voice, zero pride. I've spent my life wanting to be just like this man, wanting to make him proud, and he stands here like a damn robot. At least with me. When he calls the names of the others, the names of all the male graduates, his face lights up.

Right here and now, I make myself a promise.

I'm going to prove to him that a woman can do any fucking thing a man can do.

CHAPTER 1
CROW

I WAS BORN FOR THIS.

Present day...

"WE'VE GOT COMPANY, PRES."

I've been the president of the Soulless Kings MC: Marble Falls, TX chapter for four years now, but I still look around for my dad whenever someone says 'Pres'. I know I won't find him unless we happen to be conducting business at the cemetery and zombies suddenly become a real thing. But that doesn't seem to matter.

"Take care of 'em," I order into the coms we use on our more dangerous runs.

"Copy," Poker, my Enforcer, replies.

Poker, along with Screamer and Ghost, the club's Road Captain and Sergeant at Arms respectively, are at the back of the building so I listen for sounds of a struggle or gunfire from my position at the front.

I signal to Journey, my Vice President, to wait before entering the warehouse. We're meeting a new buyer, an MC that popped up after we obliterated the Banging Bashers MC.

Journey nods before turning to face the opposite end of the building. Several seconds later, gunshots ring out. I tense but remain in position, trusting my brothers to handle themselves.

Once the chaos dies down, both Journey and I face the door.

"All clear," Poker says, and I can hear the grin he's no doubt wearing.

"Let's do this," I respond.

Weapons drawn, Journey and I enter the building and make our way down a long hallway that opens up to the main area of the warehouse. Five men form a line in the center of the large space, and it's easy to figure out who's in charge.

"I trust that your crew handled whatever went down outside?" the man in the middle asks.

"What the fuck do you think?" I bark.

He slowly twists his head and spots Poker, Screamer, and Ghost walking toward them from behind. When he faces me again, he smirks.

"Good. I'd hate to have to find another supplier."

"There are no other suppliers."

He and I stare at one another for a long minute as if sizing each other up. Apparently satisfied with what he sees, he steps forward.

"I'm Snap, president of Limitless Throttle MC." He thrusts his hand out to shake mine. "You must be Crow."

"I am." I nod to my left. "That's Journey, my VP."

Snap tilts his head backward. "And those yahoos?"

Instant fury slams into me, and I lunge forward and wrap my hand around Snap's throat. "Disrespect me or my brothers again," I snarl. "And I'll see to it that you and yours are no more than trash in Marble Falls."

The fucker doesn't even have the decency to appear afraid. Instead, he smirks.

"And if you don't get your goddamn hand off me, I'll—"

"You'll what?" I growl, tightening my grip.

Snap slowly reaches between us and grabs my wrist and squeezes. He's stronger than he looks, but I refuse to show him my pain. Neither of us lets up for a very tense minute. He's the first to break.

He releases my wrist and raises both hands in surrender. "I meant no disrespect."

Taking a deep breath, I release him and drop my arms to my sides. "Don't make me question that again."

Snap nods curtly. "Can we get down to business now?"

Snorting, I shake my head. "You seem to think you're in charge here," I snap. "Got news for ya… You're in Soulless Kings territory. You'd do well to remember that."

He steps closer. "And you'd do well to remember that I'm not some two-bit chump off the streets looking to score. I'm the president of an MC just like you."

"Don't particularly give a fuck who you are as long as you've got money, and you don't conduct business on our turf."

Snap turns to the man on his right. "Trick, show him."

Trick, Snap's VP according to his patch, reaches into his pocket and pulls out an envelope before thrusting it at me.

"What's that?" I demand.

"Whaddya think?" Trick counters, a scowl on his lips.

"I think that's way too goddamn small to be the twenty-five grand we agreed on."

"It's all there," Snap states, his eyes boring into mine.

I yank the envelope out of Trick's hand and open it. It takes everything in me not to laugh in his face. "A check? Are you serious?" I slap the paper against Snap's chest, but he doesn't grab it. "I ain't a fuckin' bank."

In all my twenty-nine years, I've never seen an MC that deals in checks. Cash money is the only money accepted, unless it's one of the club's legitimate businesses.

And I've seen a lot. My father was the president before me, and my mother was a Bangin' Betty before becoming his ol' lady. I grew up in the club, and when the old man died, I was handed the reins.

I was born for this, and I'll be damned if I'm gonna do something that would have my dad rolling over in his grave.

"Money is money," Snap says. "It all spends the same."

"And I can't exactly take that to the bank and have them question how I got it." I glare at him while I tear the check into tiny pieces and let them fall to the floor. "You've got forty-eight hours to get me cash, or you'll have to find a different supplier."

"We're letting him walk?" Journey balks.

"I'm giving him forty-eight hours." I smirk. "We'll see if he walks after that or not."

Without saying a word, Snap shoves between Journey and me, and his brothers follow him. I turn to watch them go.

"Forty-eight hours, Snap," I call after him. "Not a second longer."

He raises his hand and flips me off. I should pull my gun and shoot him in the back but instead, I just chuckle. He has no clue who he's fucking with, but he'll find out if he tries to cross me and mine.

"Well, that was an epic waste of time."

I turn back around and face the others, but my focus is on Ghost. "Not exactly."

"Pres," Poker begins. "G's right. We got shit out of this."

"Have I taught you all nothing?" I bark.

"We got info," Journey says before I lose my patience.

"Yeah, that Limitless Throttle MC is led by a pussy," Screamer snaps. "He brought a check, dude. I mean, what the fuck was that?"

"You're right about that," I agree. "Snap doesn't have the balls to do a damn thing to SKMC. He's too soft." I grin. "And we also learned that those yahoos aren't a threat to us or our business. I'll take that info over money any day."

"They're not walking in forty-eight hours, are they?" Ghost asks.

My grin widens.

"Fuck no."

CHAPTER 2
ADDISON

I JUST WANT HIM TO TREAT ME WITH THE SAME RESPECT HE GIVES EVERYONE ELSE AND TO NOT COUNT ME OUT JUST BECAUSE I DON'T HAVE A PENIS BETWEEN MY LEGS.

"Congratulations, Detective."

Cheers erupt in the station, and I search the room for the one person who should be here, feeling defeated when I don't spot him.

"Don't take it personally."

I turn to look at Gary Stone, a man I've known for as long as I can remember. He's a hell of a detective and my dad's best friend.

"How am I supposed to do that?" I ask sadly. "This is the biggest moment of my life, and he can't even bother to show up. He's not just my dad, he's the Chief of Police. It's a slap in the face for him not to be here when I'm promoted to detective."

"You know how he gets," Gary comments. "He might not be thrilled with your career choice, but he *did* sign off on your promotion. That's gotta count for something."

I heave a sigh. "Yeah, I guess."

Gary slaps me on the back like he does with all of us. "Cheer up. This is a big day, and you should be proud of yourself."

I am proud of me. But my dad should be, too.

Gary gets pulled into a conversation with the dispatcher. Sherry's been in her position for twenty-five years, and she and Gary are close.

After another thirty minutes of mingling and ribbing from some of the officers, I return to my desk to finish clearing the space. Now that I'm a detective, I don't have to work out of the bullpen. I get my very own office.

"Here, let me help you."

I smile at Tom, but on the inside, I'm cringing. He's one of those guys who just can't take a hint. "I got it."

He reaches for the box I lifted from my desk, and I swing it out of his reach.

"C'mon, Addi," he pleads, sounding more like a

whiny teenager than an officer of the law. "It doesn't make you weak to accept a little help."

"And it doesn't make you a gentleman if you help me," I bite out.

I've spent over a year dodging Tom's advances, and he still hasn't gotten the memo. I'm not interested.

"Bitch," he mumbles under his breath as he stalks away.

I let the insult go, knowing it'll do me no good to fire back at him. Filing a complaint is out of the question because my dad would use that to argue his position that women don't belong in law enforcement.

When I step into my new office, I'm surprised to find a card propped up on a vase full of lilies on the desk. I set my box down and grab the card.

"Mom would be so proud of you," I read out loud to the empty room. "Love, Dad."

I fight back tears at the thought of my mom. She died when I was nineteen during a robbery at a gas station. She was always the one person I could count on to have my back, and losing her almost broke me.

For a few months after her death, I considered doing something with my life other than pissing my dad off by becoming a cop, but she would've been so disappointed if I didn't follow my dreams.

So, here I stand with a card in my hand instead of my dad's arms around me.

"It's true, ya know?"

I whirl around. "Dad?"

"She would've also kicked my ass for not being here on time for the big announcement."

"She would have," I agree and tilt my head. "Where were you?"

"I've been at a crime scene for the last six hours."

That piques my interest. "Oh yeah? What happened?"

"Triple homicide," he says.

"I want the case."

"I already assigned it."

Disappointment weighs me down. "To whom?"

"Stone and Briggs," he replies, referring to Gary and his partner.

"Aren't they already working several homicides?"

"They are." Dad tosses a file I didn't notice he was holding onto the desk. "Here's your first case."

The disappointment lifts slightly as I eagerly open the folder, but it doubles down when I see what kind of case he's assigning me.

"Bad checks?" I snap. "We've got several unsolved murders and a new triple homicide, and you want me to investigate a soccer mom passing bad checks?"

"Writing bad checks is fraud and a crime. Someone's gotta handle it."

"And by someone, you mean the only female detective here because surely she can't handle anything more serious."

"Addison, that's no—"

"With all due respect, *Chief*, I'd like to get going on my investigation, so if you'll excuse me…"

I turn my back to him and focus on the documents in the folder he gave me. I'm sure I'll hear about the blatant disrespect later, but I can't find it in me to care.

Dad sighs loudly, and his feet shifting on the carpet reaches my ears, so I know he's leaving.

"For what it's worth, I *am* proud of you. The fact that I'd rather you have a safer job doesn't change that."

The door quietly clicks shut a second after he utters those words, and I flop down into the chair. I know my dad loves me, and I'm sure, in his own way, he *is* proud of me. But he has absolutely no damn clue how to show me any of that.

I spend the next twenty minutes organizing my belongings, and the hour after that digging into the woman I'm assigned to investigate. I could've dug up the info I found in ten minutes, but my mind kept wandering to the triple homicide.

I'm so lost in thought about how I can get in on the case that I don't realize my office door is open until a throat is cleared.

I lift my head and see Gary smirking at me. He tips his head to indicate the computer. "Anything good?"

"If you consider fraud good, yeah, sure," I huff out.

He turns to close the door, and when he faces me again, there's sympathy in his eyes. "I'm sorry, Addi," Gary says. "He'll come around."

"I'm not so sure about that, Uncle G," I say, reverting to the name I've called him since I was a little girl. "The only thing I've ever wanted is to follow in his footsteps, and all he wants is to lock me away in a padded room."

"Can you blame him?"

I narrow my eyes. "I'm a grown woman. He can't protect me forever."

Gary lowers his gaze. "Your mother was a grown woman, too, and he'd give anything to have been able to protect her."

I stiffen at his words. "Don't. Don't you dare bring Mom into this. He started treating me like I wasn't good enough long before she was killed."

"I know, but that certainly didn't help."

He's right about that. "Look, I just want him to

treat me with the same respect he gives everyone else and not count me out just because I don't have a penis between my legs."

"Then prove to him that you are as good, if not better, than the rest of us."

"I thought that's what I've been doing," I counter.

Gary leans forward, resting his palms on my desk. "I could use another detective on this triple homicide. Whaddya say? Wanna help me out?"

"And go behind Chief's back?"

Gary shrugs. "Some rules were meant to be broken."

This is why I love him. He's always had the same belief as my mom: I can do anything I set my mind to. He's just a bit more careful voicing that opinion in front of my dad.

"Then let's break them."

CHAPTER 3
CROW

THIS FEELS DIFFERENT.

"WHAT CAN I GET YA?"

Conner, the prospect working the bar tonight, is young and eager to please. He had a shit childhood which means he has a lot of anger to work through. But he's a good kid and will be an asset to the club… when he's ready.

"Shot of Jack," I reply. "Ya know what? Just give me the whole damn bottle and a shot glass."

"You sure about that, Pres?" Conner asks.

I reach across the bar and grab ahold of his shirt to yank him toward me. "Don't ever fucking question me," I snarl. "Got it?"

"Got it."

He stumbles backward when I shove him away

and then he quickly whirls around to grab the bottle of Jack Daniels. Conner hands me the booze before wisely retreating to clean some imaginary mess.

I carry the bottle to the recliner I positioned in the corner of the room and flop down. Sitting here, I can see everything which is just how I like it.

"What crawled up your ass?"

Slowly, I lift my gaze and glare at Journey. "Nothing."

"Bullshit," he snaps. "The only time you take the whole bottle is when something's eating at you. So, spit it out."

I don't say a word as I stare at him, silently berating him for daring to interrupt my alcohol-fueled pity party of one.

"Oh, I see," he says calmly as he sits on the couch against the wall. "You're freaking out because of those three Limitless Throttle brothers."

When we returned to the warehouse for the forty-eight-hour deadline, Snap, Trick, and another of their patched members were gutted like animals in the middle of the building. And if they brought the cash, it was long gone.

"I'm not freaking out," I snap.

"Fine," he capitulates. "But you can't ignore the problem their deaths create for us."

"No shit."

"We'll figure it all out," my VP says. "We always do."

"And while we do that, do you really think the cops are gonna give a damn that we had nothing to do with it?"

"They can't pin murders on us that we didn't commit."

"They can, and they will."

"Crow, we've got an inside man for a reason," he reminds me. "He'll make sure we're left out of the investigation."

I grunt in response. Journey's right, we do have a cop on our payroll. But sometimes, even all the money in the world can't penetrate that thin blue line.

"Why don't you go bang out your anger?" he suggests, nodding toward Molly, one of the Bangin' Betties. "She's always up for a little sexual punishment."

"Not in the mood."

"Since when?"

"Since my head isn't in the game."

Journey throws his head back and laughs. "Not touching that with a ten-foot pole."

I throw the shot glass at him, and it bounces off his chest and falls to the floor where it shatters. "Shut the fuck up."

He glances over his shoulder and shouts at a prospect. "Blain, come clean this shit up!"

"On it," Blain calls back as he rushes toward the closet to get the broom.

Then Journey refocuses on me. "Pres, we're gonna be fine."

Again, I grunt in response, and he walks away instead of pushing the issue further. There's nothing left to say. Journey is the best VP I could ask for, and his willingness to disagree with me is why. He'll follow my orders, but he also calls me on my shit.

Deciding to take his advice, I rise from the chair and step around Blain as he reaches the broken glass and starts to sweep. I cross the floor, my sights set on Molly.

Maybe banging out my anger will do the trick.

"Hey, Crow," Molly purrs when I stop in front of her. She reaches out and flattens her palm against my chest. "What can I do for ya?"

I take a swig from the bottle I've still got clutched in my hand before grabbing her wrist and dragging her toward the stairs.

Molly's heels click on the steps, the sound sharp and annoying. It's on the tip of my tongue to demand she take them off, but I keep the words to myself.

"You seem to be in a bit of a hurry," Molly comments, her voice breathy.

"If I wanted to talk, I'd talk," I snap, hoping she gets the hint to shut the fuck up.

When I reach my room, I stride inside, kicking the door closed behind us. I turn her around so she's facing the barrier and push her against it. After setting the open bottle of Jack Daniels on my dresser, I hike her skimpy leather skirt up to her waist and tune out her begging for my cock.

Five minutes later, Molly's crying and scrambling to get out of my room. I yank my zipper up but leave the button of my jeans undone, then grab the booze before making my way to the bed. I've never not been able to get it up for her, or any woman for that matter.

All the Limitless Throttle bullshit really has me in my head. It's not like we haven't dealt with stuff like this before. Hell, we eliminated the Bangin' Bashers MC, and our law enforcement contact handled the fallout for us, but…

This feels different.

For the next hour, I drown my worries in alcohol. My head swims, and my vision blurs, but I don't pass out like I hope. Instead, my concerns refuse to sink without a fight.

Will the police come for us?
What evidence will be found at the crime scene?
Will every last clue point in our direction?

How will I protect the club?

Who the fuck killed those bikers?

My cell pings, pulling me out of my thoughts, and I take it out of my cut pocket and stare at the screen.

> Oinker: Search warrant signed for clubhouse… coming in an hour

The alcohol-induced haze I've been in immediately disappears. I quickly get to my feet and bolt out of my room. While I'm running down the steps, I fire off a quick text.

> Me: Thanks 4 the warning

> Oinker: Have my $$ ready

I groan. Not only do I have to get this place ready to be torn apart, but I also have to worry about handing over a bribe in the middle of a sea of cops.

Asshole.

"Rise and shine!" I shout as I make my way through the clubhouse, banging on doors. "Code blue!"

Within minutes, everyone is gathered in the main room.

"Judge signed a search warrant," I begin. "And apparently, they think coming in the middle of the night is gonna work in their favor. Let's get this place ready and prove them wrong."

By the time the swarm of police and detectives arrive, there isn't a shred of anything illegal to be found.

CHAPTER 4
ADDISON

And just like that, things are looking up.

"Not a damn thing."

I lean against the edge of my desk and cross my arms over my chest. Gary stormed into the room a few minutes ago, and he's been pacing like a lion that's dying to get out of a cage.

"Seriously?"

"We searched the entire place. No weapons, no drugs, no sign of anything illegal beyond the smug look on all their faces while they watched us tear their place apart."

"Maybe they didn't do it," I say, but my tone lacks conviction.

There's absolutely zero chance that the Soulless Kings MC didn't take out those other bikers.

Everyone within a hundred-mile radius of Marble Falls knows they're into some shady shit. Sure, they own several businesses that help the town's economy, but that doesn't make them any less criminal.

"If you believe that, then maybe your dad is right," Gary mutters.

Shock washes over me, and if the desk weren't holding me up, I'd stumble under the weight of it. Gary's never made me feel like I wasn't good enough.

I must not be good at hiding my emotions because he stops pacing and frowns. "I'm sorry, Addi. I didn't mean that."

"It's, uh…" I run my hands through my long hair. "It's okay. But I really need to get back to this fraud case."

"Right." Gary walks to the door but pauses before exiting. "If you need any help, let me know. And if you think of anything on my case, I'm all ears."

Without waiting for a reply, he leaves me alone with my thoughts. I spend the rest of my shift putting together all the info I've gathered on the fraud case. Turns out, the woman wasn't just passing bad checks. She's also the treasurer of her son's soccer league—*Oh yeah, she really is a soccer mom*—, and she's stealing from that pot of money in an effort to cover said checks. Newsflash lady, it ain't working.

At six o'clock, my phone pings with a text. I glance at the screen and grin.

> Mona: Time's up detective. You're done for the day. Now get your ass to the bar. We've got some drinkin to do

> Me: Yes ma'am. See ya in 30

Mona and I have remained best friends since grade school, and we make a point to hang out at least one Friday night a month. And tonight is that Friday night.

I gather my stuff and head to the locker room to change into something more appropriate for a bar. After applying more makeup and switching from my pants suit to jeans and a black top with tall black boots, I make my way to my car in the lot behind the precinct.

Exactly thirty-four minutes later, I park next to Mona's vehicle outside of Ballinger's Bar. Her car is empty, and I can only hope that she's already ordered me a shot of Fireball and a beer.

As soon as I step inside, I'm instantly in a better mood. Southern rock blares from the jukebox, and the crowd is hyped up with the end of another work week. I spot Mona standing at the bar, and when she sees me, she waves me over.

"Here ya go," she says, handing me a full shot glass before I even have a chance to say 'hi'.

I take the alcohol and down it, letting the liquid burn a path to my gut, and then lean close to her ear. "I need more."

Mona grins. "Comin' right up!"

Once the bartender has served us each two more shots, we work our way through the crowd to the one empty table in the joint.

"So, long week?" she asks after we're both seated.

I groan. "You have no idea."

"How are things going with your dad?"

I wave my hand dismissively as I take a sip of my beer. "You know how he is."

"Uptight and sexist?"

"Watch it," I say, but there's no heat in my tone. "Those things may be true, but he's still my dad."

Mona lifts her hands apologetically. "You know I love the old guy, Addi. Hell, he's practically my second father. I just wish he saw in you what the rest of the world sees."

"Oh yeah? And what's that?"

"That you're amazing and can do anything you put your mind to."

"Thanks."

This isn't the first time we've had this conversation, and I know it won't be the last. I just wish it never even had to happen.

"How's Patrick?" I ask her in an effort to avoid more conversation about my dad's lack of faith in me.

Mona groans. "We broke up."

"What? When?"

Patrick only moved in with Mona a month ago, but they'd been together for two years.

"Last night."

"What happened?"

"He was fucking the neighbor."

My eyes widen. "That red-headed chick in the green house?"

"That's the one."

I wrinkle my nose. "Damn."

"I came home from work early and found them in bed together," she says. Mona takes a long sip of her beer before continuing. "By the way, do you have time to go bed shopping this weekend? I need a new one."

Laughter bubbles up the back of my throat and comes out as a snort. "Sure. I'm off all weekend. Do you want me to be at the house when he comes to get his stuff?"

"What stuff?"

"Mona?" I arch a brow. "What did you do?"

She shrugs. "If he wants his stuff, he should probably bring a shovel because it's all a pile of ash in the burn barrel."

"You didn't?"

She smirks. "I did. And don't you dare go all cop on me. The prick cheated."

"Wasn't gonna go all cop," I tell her honestly. "In fact, I was gonna ask if you wanted help burying the body."

"Damn, whose body are we buryin' ladies?"

Mona and I had been so lost in conversation that we didn't realize someone had walked up to our table. I open my mouth to tell him to get lost, but I don't get any words out before Mona speaks.

"Why? You gonna help us?" she asks, her tone turning silky smooth.

Oh shit.

The man grins. "That could be arranged."

"Well then…" Mona nods to the seat next to her. "Have a seat."

If I didn't know her like I do, I'd think she was about to arrange for a hit on Patrick.

"I'm Blain," the man says.

"Mona." My best friend glances at me. "And that's Addison."

"So, who's about to be six feet under?"

"My ex," Mona replies.

"Ah, so you're single?" Blain asks.

"I am." She darts her eyes from Blain to me and back again. "We both are."

Dammit.

"Then how about instead of getting your pretty little hands dirty, you both come to a party tomorrow night?"

"No, tha—"

"Where at?" Mona asks, talking over me.

"Have you heard of the Soulless Kings?" Blain asks, and the hair on the back of my neck stands on end.

"Kinda hard to grow up in Marble Falls and not hear about them," I comment.

"Well, the party's at their clubhouse," Blain explains. He puffs up his chest like a proud peacock. "I'm prospecting with them."

It takes every ounce of willpower I possess not to scream 'we'll be there'. As much as I would rather stay home and watch Netflix, this invitation couldn't have come at a more perfect time.

"Addi, whaddya say?" Mona asks. "Wanna go?"

Yes, yes, yes!

I shrug, feigning indifference. "Up to you. You're the one who just got out of a long-term relationship."

Mona rolls her eyes, but then she grins and returns her attention to Blain. "We're in."

"Perfect." Blain pulls out his cell. "What's your number?" he asks Mona.

She rattles off the digits, and a second later, her cell pings.

"That's the address," he tells her. "Party starts at nine."

And just like that, things are looking up.

CHAPTER 5
CROW

As a child, she was an enigma, but as an adult, Addison McGill is a problem.

"Some things never change."

I glance at Ghost, surprised to see him. "What're you still doing here?"

"I'm heading out in a few," he says. "Wanted to hang a bit though, especially after the week we've had."

The party is in full swing so I'm grateful he doesn't elaborate. I know he's referring to the three dead bikers and the search of the clubhouse.

I lift my beer bottle and tap the neck of his. "Nothing like this ever happened in Oregon?"

Ghost transferred into our chapter a little over a year ago and quickly earned his patch and title of

Sergeant at Arms. I was surprised when he took me up on my invitation to return to Texas, but then he explained that his mother was sick, and he was coming home to care for her.

"Plenty of shit happened," he admits. "But I don't have time to get into those stories."

I chuckle. "Got it."

"Well, I'm gonna head out. It's Nancy's night off, and I don't want Mom to be alone too long."

"How is she?" I ask. "Your mom, not Nancy."

"There's good days and bad days," he says with a sigh.

"Nancy still the only help you have?" I ask, referring to the home health nurse Ghost hired.

"Not many nurses in Marble Falls specialize in Alzheimer's care so yeah, she's it."

"You know if you need anything, all ya gotta do is ask, right?"

"Thanks, Pres. Appreciate that."

"Hey, we're family. It's what we do."

"And that's a sentence I never thought I'd hear outta Trace Thompson's mouth," Ghost says with a laugh.

"It's Crow," I snap.

"Yeah, yeah." Ghost slaps me on the back. "I'm outta here. See ya tomorrow."

"Be safe," I call after him. "And give your mom a hug for me."

Ghost lifts his hand in response, and I watch as he walks out the door of the clubhouse, his steps a little heavier than usual.

I head to the pool tables where Journey is battling Screamer.

"I've got the winner," I announce.

Fifteen minutes later, Screamer sinks the eight ball.

"Son of a bitch!" Journey shouts.

"Don't be such a twat," Screamer taunts as he holds his hand out. "Pay up, loser."

Journey reaches into his pocket and pulls out his wallet. He slaps a hundred-dollar bill into Screamer's palm before stalking toward the bar.

"He really hates to lose," I comment dryly as I lift his discarded cue.

Screamer chuckles. "Don't we all?"

"Yeah, we do," I agree. "So how about I kick your ass, and you be the sore loser this time?"

"Two hundred says I win," he counters.

I reach into my wallet and slap two crisp hundreds onto the side of the pool table. "You're on."

I rack the balls and let my road captain take the first shot. He sinks the eleven ball but misses his second shot.

"Looks like I'm gonna make an easy two hundred," I say as I line up my shot.

I pull my arm back and—

"Yo, Crow!"

I miss the cue ball completely. Rage blurs my vision as I whirl around and face the prospect who interrupted my shot.

"I swear to God, Conner, this had better be a fucking emergency," I snarl.

"We've got a problem at the door, Pres," he says. "Poker told me to come get you."

I toss the cue onto the table, sending balls going in every direction. Then I snatch up my cash.

"Uh, that's not how this works, bro," Screamer comments.

"I'll be back, and we'll go another round, double or nothing," I reply, and that seems to satisfy him. Focusing my attention on Conner, I follow him to the door. "What the fuck is the problem?"

"Some bitch is raising hell because Poker tried to take her gun," Conner explains.

"Tried?"

Conner laughs. "Yeah, tried. She put him on his ass the second he touched the weapon."

"Jesus," I say with a sigh.

Commotion reaches my ears as we get closer, and when I step just outside the door, I freeze.

Poker has a woman pinned against the brick wall, and she looks very familiar. She's sexy as hell with her long chestnut brown hair framing her nearly perfect face. There's another woman shouting at him to 'get his filthy hands' off her friend, but she's a redhead and not nearly as stunning.

Who is she? Where do I know her from?

"Let her go," I command.

Poker shifts his gaze to me and frowns. "Pres?"

"Let her go," I repeat.

He drops his hands, and the woman brushes hers down the front of her black leather jacket. My eyes follow the movement, and my cock hardens at the way her hips flare slightly beneath skin-tight denim.

"Now, what the fuck is going on?" I demand, not bothering to take my stare away from her body.

"Bitch has a Glock in a holster under her jacket," Poker states, annoyed.

"That true?" I ask her.

"And if it is?"

"No weapons allowed inside."

"Yet you've got one under that shirt of yours," she says coolly. "And you've got a knife tucked into your boot."

I arch a brow, impressed. "You seem to know an awful lot."

"I'm observant."

"Right."

"Look," her friend says, stepping forward. "Blain invited us to the party. We don't want any trouble."

"Then tell her to hand over her gun," Poker snaps.

"P, go inside and grab a drink," I instruct. "I'll handle this."

Poker stares at me for a long moment, but then he does as he's told. Conner stays back a few steps, and I nod toward the door, silently telling him to get lost. He strides inside, letting the door slam closed behind him.

When I return my attention to the women, they're both staring at me expectantly. I take a step toward them, and the redhead shifts closer to her gun-carrying friend.

"What's your name?" I ask the one who was pinned to the wall.

"What's yours?" she counters, crossing her arms over her chest.

Her cleavage pillows over the edge of her top, and my mouth waters.

"My name is Trace," I say, not bothering to speculate as to why I'm giving her my legal name. "But everyone calls me Crow."

She nods. "I'm Addison."

The second her name passes her lips, a memory

slams into me.

"Class, please welcome Trace Thompson."

I stare at the other kids as they size me up. This is the last place I want to be, but my dad didn't give me a choice. Since my mom died, there's no one left at home to teach me.

Apparently, I need an education. It doesn't seem to matter that I'll take over the club one day.

"Trace, you can have a seat right there," Ms. Cochran says, pointing to an empty desk. "That's Addison McGill, and she'll be your buddy for the next few days to help you get acclimated."

Addison McGill is really pretty, but she looks upset about something. I move through the rows of desks until I reach mine. Instead of sitting, I face Addison.

"What's wrong with you?" I ask.

She glares at me. "Nothing."

"Are you mad because you're supposed to be my buddy?"

"No."

"Mr. Thompson," Ms. Cochran chastises. "Have a seat so we can get back to work."

I sit as instructed, but instead of listening to the teacher drone on about state capitals, I watch Addison out of the corner of my eye. She's drawing on a piece of paper, and I recognize the shape: handcuffs.

I shake my head to force myself to return to the

present. After my first day in public school, I made a point to learn everything I could about Addison McGill. She was the prettiest girl in my class and somewhat of a mystery.

But one thing she couldn't hide was her love for her father and what he did for a living. She idolized the man. It was easy for me to figure that out because I was the same way with my own dad.

Both of us wanted nothing more than to make our dads see us and believe in us.

The biggest difference was that we came from very different worlds. She grew up on the side of right, and I on the side of wrong… ish.

And now she's at my clubhouse, staring at me very intently. As a child, she was an enigma, but as an adult, Addison McGill is a problem.

I can't tell if she knows that I know who she is, but that doesn't matter. There's no way she's leaving the property tonight. Hell, I don't know if I'll ever let her leave.

I force a smile while I'm burning with rage on the inside. Are the police really so desperate to pin those biker's murders on us that they'll send someone undercover?

Reaching out, I gently urge Addison toward the door.

"C'mon in and enjoy the party."

CHAPTER 6
ADDISON

Don't all Texans feel naked without a weapon?

C'mon in and enjoy the party.

Crow's words bang around in my brain like little silver balls in a pinball machine. When he introduced himself, I recognized him immediately. But he must not remember me, or I wouldn't currently be sitting at the bar inside the clubhouse.

In the middle of the lion's den.

"Can I get you another beer?"

I turn away from watching Mona dance with Blain and smile at the bartender. "Sure."

Less than a minute later, a second bottle is set in front of me.

"Not gonna dance with your friend?"

"Maybe in a bit," I say. "She seems to be having fun without me right now."

"That she does." The bartender chuckles. "I'm Kenny."

"Addison."

"I know," Kenny says matter-of-factly. When I glare at him, he shrugs. "You're the chick who tried to get a gun in here. News travels fast through the clubhouse."

My blood boils at the reminder that Crow relieved me of my weapon the second we crossed the threshold. I couldn't exactly continue to put up a fight without raising suspicion, so I let him have it.

"So, Blain invited you and your friend tonight?" Kenny asks.

"Yeah."

"You're not very talkative, are you?"

Not when I'm trying to observe every detail around me.

"Sorry," I say. "Just tired I guess."

"Then drink up, buttercup," he encourages. "Nothing wakes you up quite like a good buzz."

"If that's the case, where'd the term 'whiskey dick' come from?" I counter.

Kenny snorts with laughter. "I like you, Addison."

"Thanks."

I don't know how I feel about that. Maybe I could use it to my advantage and get him to talk, but something tells me Kenny is tight-lipped.

"Addi!"

I lift my hand to wave at Mona, but she shakes her head and runs toward me.

"You're dancing… now," she demands as she drags me into the crowd.

"Mona, I'm not nearly drunk enough for this," I protest.

"That's no excuse." She pouts, knowing full well that's how to get me to cave. "C'mon, have a little fun."

I'm not here for fun. I'm here for work.

But I keep that thought to myself. After chugging half the bottle in my hand, I begin to let the music guide my actions. I sway to the beat and do my best to blend in.

"Looks like you've got a fan," Mona says after a few minutes.

I follow her gaze and spot Crow sitting in a recliner, his eyes focused on me. He lifts his glass in salute, and I plaster a smile on my face. Apparently, smiling is some sort of invitation because he stands and stalks toward me.

The man is insanely hot, and my insides twist as I

take in the sight of him. Fucking hell, if he weren't such a horrible person, I'd really let loose tonight.

"Enjoying yourself?" he asks, leaning close to my ear to be heard over the music.

His breath skates across my cheek, and I shiver.

Stop it, Addi!

"I'd be having more fun if I had my gun," I snap, annoyed at the effect he seems to have on me.

Crow leans back to look me in the eyes. "Why do you want it so bad?"

"I'm from Texas. Don't all Texans feel naked without a weapon?"

He grins, and his gray eyes flash with mischief. "You feel naked?" His voice is deep, gravelly… sexy.

"If I took your weapons, wouldn't you?" I counter, trying like hell to not let him see what he's doing to me.

"Touché."

Arms wrap around me from behind, and Mona's perfume fills my senses.

"I'm gonna go sit for a minute," she says. "You good?"

I don't take my eyes off Crow as I nod.

"Don't do anything I wouldn't do," she instructs cheerfully.

Crow arches a brow. "And what wouldn't she do?"

"There isn't much," I admit. "She's on the rebound."

"And you?"

"And me what?"

"Are you spoken for?"

My brain screams at me to tell him I am, to give him the name of some fake boyfriend, but my mouth doesn't cooperate.

"No."

Dammit.

"Interesting," he drawls.

Before he can take the conversation any further, one of his buddies steps up next to him and whispers something in his ear. Crow listens intently, his stare never leaving me, and then he nods.

"Addison, I've got something to take care of," he says when his friend walks away. "Enjoy the rest of the party."

With that, he disappears into the sea of people. I glance around and realize that it's now or never. If I'm going to find any dirt on the Soulless Kings, I need to act.

"Excuse me," I say as I tap a woman's shoulder.

"What?" she snaps.

"Where's the bathroom?"

She points to the other side of the room. "Down that hall, second door on the right."

"Thanks."

I make my way toward the hall, paying close attention to if anyone is watching me. When I reach the second door on the right, it's closed.

"Gimme a fuckin' minute," a man snaps when I knock.

A woman's giggle follows his voice, and I roll my eyes. I guess I should be grateful that they're behind a closed door.

While I wait, I lean against the wall and cross my arms over my chest. Several bikers walk past me, but none of them say a word or even seem to realize I'm standing there. And I'm okay with that. Makes it easier to do my job.

Five minutes later, the bathroom door bangs open and the man who pinned me against the wall strolls out. Two almost naked women follow him. The smell of booze and marijuana fills the air as they walk by me, and I wrinkle my nose against it.

I duck inside and lock the door behind me. A quick glance in the mirror reveals flushed cheeks, but I don't stop to analyze why.

A certain biker, perhaps?

After pouring my beer out in the sink, I take the time to search the medicine cabinet and drawers in the vanity. Nothing stands out that I could use to make a case against the club. I didn't exactly expect to find anything in here, but it never hurts to look.

Frustrated, I return to the party and look for Mona. She's dancing with a guy I don't recognize, and she seems to be having fun, so I leave her to it.

I walk to the bar to get another beer. As soon as Kenny hands one to me, I start to mingle with the party guests, making small talk with anyone I can.

How else am I going to find dirt on the club?

CHAPTER 7
CROW

Electricity zaps each and every one of my nerve endings until I'm aware of nothing but her.

"She's got balls, I'll give her that."

I down my latest shot of Jack while my gaze remains on Addison. She's currently dancing with Python. When my brother wraps his arm around her waist and pulls her to his chest, jealousy slithers through my system.

She might be the enemy, but my foe has never looked so enticing.

"We'll see how big those balls are when she finds herself stuck here." I smirk at Journey. "Gather the officers and meet me in church. Do it quietly."

While my second-in-command gathers the others, I spare Addison one last look before making my way to the meeting room. I don't bother taking my weapons out and putting them in the box outside the door.

"Damn, Pres," Screamer grumbles when he enters the room. "I was just about to take Sunny upstairs."

"She's not goin' anywhere," I snap. "You can have your fun when we're done."

"What's this about, bro?" Poker asks when he walks in.

I pull out my cell and call Ghost on Facetime. He's an officer and needs to be a part of the vote I'm about to pose.

"Yo, Pres, everything okay?" Ghost asks when he answers.

"No. I've called the officers together for a vote," I explain.

"A vote?" Poker asks. "For what?"

I heave a sigh. "Ghost, I'm gonna send you a pic I took of a woman at the party tonight. I need you to confirm my suspicions."

"Okay."

I open my photos and select the one I took of Addison earlier. After sending it, I wait. Ghost remains quiet.

"Well?" Journey prods. "Is it her?"

"Would someone please fil—"

"Jesus, how'd she get in?" Ghost barks, ignoring Screamer.

"How did who get in?" Poker demands. "What the fuck is going on?"

I scowl. "Addison McGill, daughter of the Chief of Police, is out there right now," I snarl, pointing at the door.

"Fucking hell," Screamer barks. "This is bad."

"No shit," I snap. "Do you really think I'd call you away from a party if it wasn't?"

"What's the vote, Pres?" Journey asks.

"With everything going on with the dead Limitless Throttle brothers, I don't think it's a coincidence that she's here," I say. "I wanna keep her here."

"You wanna abduct the Chief of Police's daughter?" Poker asks skeptically.

"Do you have a better idea?" I counter. "Because our clubhouse was searched the other day, and clearly the police think we're responsible for those murders. She's gonna find something tonight. Maybe not connected to murder, but there's all sorts of illegal shit going down."

"Will she ever walk out of here?" Journey asks.

"That depends," I reply honestly. "If she cooperates and agrees to do so in the future, we'll let her go… eventually."

"And if she doesn't cooperate?" Ghost asks.

"Then we do whatever we fucking have to." I take a deep breath. "All those in favor of keeping Ms. McGill here, thump twice."

My brothers each bang their fists on the table twice. And since he's on the phone, Ghost presses a button two times for his vote.

"Vote passes," I say. "Journey, go see if Kenny still has any of that shit we found on him the night we took him in. Screamer, get Python and fill him in. Let him know that I need him to keep Addison occupied and supplied with booze."

"Whaddya want me to do?" Poker asks.

"I need you to get with Blain and between the two of you, get Addison's friend out of here. I have no interest in holding her hostage as well."

"And me, Pres?" Ghost asks.

"You stay with your mom until the nurse gets back," I tell him. "We've got things handled here." I glance around the room and grin. "Let's get to it."

With church over, my brothers return to the party. I have all the confidence in the world that they'll carry out orders. None of them have ever let me down, and I don't expect they'll start now. Not with something this important.

I make my way back to the common room and cut my gaze to the bar. Journey is talking to Kenny, and I watch them closely. While I need Kenny to have the drugs necessary to knock Addison out, a part of me hopes he doesn't since he was instructed to never use them again.

When Kenny reaches into his pocket and hands Journey a small plastic baggie, I sigh. Looks like Addison won't be the only one in the Nightmare Room tonight.

Journey hands the baggie back to Kenny and gives him instructions. I didn't specify during church what I wanted done with them, but it doesn't take a genius to figure it out.

Once I'm satisfied that Addison's next drink will be spiked, I search the room for Screamer. He's speaking to Python, who's nodding with a giant grin on his face. No doubt, he's thrilled to be responsible for keeping Addison close.

Next, I look for Poker. He's in the middle of the dance floor with Blain and Mona. His job should be fairly easy if the way Mona is staggering is any indication. She's already way past drunk. It shouldn't be too hard to convince her that it's time to go home.

I head to my recliner and sit. As I always do, I watch as everything unfolds. It's not thirty minutes later that Blain is carrying Mona outside. There was a brief conversation between Mona and Addison and apparently, Addison wasn't ready to head out just yet.

Shocker... Can't very well get dirt on us if she leaves.

My attention settles on Addison and Python. When the song changes, he stops dancing and practically drags her to the bar. Kenny serves them both a fresh beer, and I know it won't be long now.

I stand and cross the room.

"We've got a problem, prospect," I say calmly when I reach the bar.

"I know," Kenny says. "I can't believe that bit—"

"Wasn't referring to her," I snap and reach across the bar to grab a handful of his shirt and yank him toward me. "You were told to get rid of that shit."

His face pales. "I... I know. But aren't you glad I didn't listen?"

"We'd have found another way."

"And now you don't have to," he argues.

"You're right," Journey states when he steps up next to me. "But you still disobeyed orders, and that can't go unpunished."

"Unpunished?" Kenny repeats. "What're ya gonna do?"

The fear in his tone sends adrenaline coursing through my veins. Without letting him go, I glance over my shoulder.

"Conner!" I shout to be heard over the music. "Get behind the bar."

Conner scurries to do my bidding. "Need me to take over, Pres?"

"Yes," I reply, returning my attention back to Kenny. "You're headed downstairs."

"Oh shit," Conner quips while shaking his head.

"VP, get him outta my sight," I demand.

Journey walks around the bar and wraps his meaty hand around Kenny's bicep. He drags him to the hall that leads to the steel door. I'll deal with the prospect later. Right now, I need to focus on getting Addison downstairs as well.

My eyes land on Addison, who's taking a long pull from her beer.

Won't be long now.

After a few minutes, and several more sips, Addison begins to sway, and not to the beat of the music. Her knees buckle, and Python quickly scoops her into his arms. That evil green monster reappears, and I rush forward.

"Give her to me," I demand when I reach the pair.

Python wisely keeps his mouth shut and hands her over. I carry Addison through the crowd, and no one gives us a second glance. As far as they're concerned, I'm carrying a chick who can't hold her liquor to a room so she can sleep it off.

Addison is light in my arms despite essentially being dead weight. My fingers dig into her flesh where her shirt crept up, and touching her is like a lightning strike. Electricity zaps each and every one of my nerve endings until I'm aware of nothing but her.

"Let me outta here!"

Kenny's shout pulls me from my trance. Journey is standing just outside the door to the Nightmare Room, watching Kenny on the monitor.

"Open the door," I order Journey. "Then get me the cot."

He presses the button on the wall, and the door slides open. While I carry Addison inside, Journey moves to the storage room. Kenny continues to shout, but I tune him out.

"Here ya go," Journey says when he returns with the cot and a blanket thrown over his shoulder.

"Put it against the wall," I say, nodding to where I want the bed. I glance at Kenny. "You touch this thing, and you won't walk out of here on your own, got it?"

That seems to shut him up. He nods.

I lay Addison down and grab the blanket Journey hands me. After I cover her up, Journey and I retreat out of the room, and the door slides closed.

"Now what?" Journey asks.

I grin. "Now we wait."

CHAPTER 8
ADDISON

If I run, I have nothing.

My head pounds as consciousness seeps in. I roll onto my side and force my eyes open. Panic hits me hard, and I sit up so fast my vision blurs.

"You're awake."

I lift my head and stare at Kenny. He's sitting across the room with his back against the wall.

"What did you do to me?" I ask, my mouth dry.

He chuckles, but there's no humor in it. "I didn't do shit."

I run a hand through my hair and groan. "Why can't I... What happened?"

Before he can answer, the door to the concrete room slides open, and a man I don't recognize walks in.

"He's lying to you," the man says.

Confusion laces my mind. I have no recollection of what happened last night and no clue who I can trust.

You went undercover at the Soulless Kings clubhouse. You can't trust anyone.

"I'm Ghost," the man says as he crouches next to the cot. "And you're Addison McGill."

"How do you know who I am?"

"Kenny put Rohypnol in your beer," Ghost says matter-of-factly. "That's the—"

"Date rape drug," I spit out as I curl in on myself. "Yeah, I know."

"You weren't raped," Ghost comments. "I hope that makes you feel a little better."

Outrage spikes in my blood. "Feel better? Feel fucking better?!" I jump to my feet, and the blanket that was covering me falls to the floor. I'm still fully clothed, and that slightly dampens my temper. "I was still drugged and locked in, in, this—"

"They call it the Nightmare Room."

I swivel my neck to gawk at Kenny, who's now standing. "The what?"

"Kenny, shut the fuck up," Ghost barks.

"Why?" Kenny asks. "I'm in here too. Pretty sure I've got nothing to lose at this point."

"What's he talking about?" I demand.

"Kenny screwed up." Ghost shrugs. "And we don't take screw ups lightly."

"Journey told me to put it in her drink!" Kenny shouts.

I press my forefingers against my temples. The headache I woke up with is worsening by the second.

"Why did you come here?" Ghost asks me.

"My friend and—" I press my lips together for a long moment. "Where the hell is Mona?"

"I assume she's at home."

"You assume?"

"Blain was ordered to see her home safely last night," Ghost explains. "Not sure if she's a church goin' woman or likes to take a morning run so I can't say whether or not she's still at her apartment."

"Why keep me and not her?"

Ghost tilts his head. "Do you really need to ask that?"

"She wouldn't be very good at her job if she didn't ask questions."

I lift my eyes to the doorway and see Crow standing there with a smug expression.

"If you know who I am and what I do, why keep me? Why risk it?"

"We're not risking anything," Crow states as he strides toward me.

Shit.

"You've got someone on the inside," I deduce.

"Score one for the detective," Crow taunts.

"You won't get away with this," I seethe.

"We'll see about that." Crow shifts his attention to Kenny. "As for you…"

"Bro, I didn—"

Crow advances on Kenny and shoves him against the wall. "I'm not your bro," he snarls. "You were a prospect, nothing more."

Kenny lifts his hands. "Fine, whatever. But the fact remains that she wouldn't still be here if I had listened to you."

"Which is why you get to live," Ghost says from his position near me.

"Wait, what?" I demand. "You'd kill him over this?"

Crow glances over his shoulder. "For bringing a drug into my clubhouse that's designed to hurt women? Yeah, I'd fucking kill him."

"But you used it on me," I remind him.

"Which is why he gets to walk away," Crow says with exaggerated patience. "I'm not a monster."

I snort. "Right. You're just a man who orchestrated my drugging and kidnapping."

"No, Addi. I'm a man who will do what is necessary to protect those he loves."

"My name is Addison."

"It is," he agrees. "But Addi suits you better."

I huff out a breath, exasperated. Going verbal rounds with a criminal isn't exactly what I had in mind for my day, but then again, waking up unaware of what happened in the last twelve hours or so wasn't either.

"I should insist on you calling me 'detective'," I grumble.

"Look around, Ace. You're not exactly in a position to be calling the shots."

"Ace?"

Crow shrugs. "That's as close to 'detective' that you'll get from me." He returns his attention to Kenny. "As for you... Ghost is gonna walk you upstairs and watch as you clean out your shit from the prospect room. Then he's gonna escort you outside, and you're gonna get the fuck off my property. Remember, Kenny, if you run your mouth, I'll permanently close it for you."

Crow yanks him away from the wall and pushes him toward Ghost. The two of them walk out of the room, and the Soulless Kings' president stalks to me.

"Contrary to what you might think," he begins. "I don't like what I'm having to do here. I'd much rather you be in my presence by choice than force."

"That'll never happen."

"Maybe, but time will tell." Crow extends his arm and brushes a strand of hair behind my ear. I know I should dodge his touch, but my body doesn't obey my silent command. "For now, I'll settle on you learning that we're not bad men."

"You're drug dealers, murderers, and God only knows what else."

"We're also a family," he counters. "Loyal, loving, charitable, honest, and passionate."

"Right. And keeping me here against my will proves all that," I snark.

"No. That act doesn't prove shit. But you spending time around us, around me, will show you that we're not guilty of the crime you want to pin on us."

"I don't want to pin anything on you. I want to arrest you for murder."

"We didn't murder anyone."

"What about the Limitless Throttle MC guys?" I ask. "The evidence points to you and your brothers. I can't ignore evidence."

"The evidence was staged."

I throw my head back and laugh. "That's what everyone says."

"I'm sure they do. But unlike most of them, I'm telling the truth."

"Prove it."

"That, *Ace*, is why you're here."

"And here I thought we were gonna have a sleepover and do each other's nails."

Crow's eye twitches with annoyance. "Being a smart ass isn't going to earn you a lot of goodwill."

"Sorry. It's not in my DNA to do anything else."

He tilts his head and stares at me as if studying a specimen under a microscope. "That's not the Addison I remember. You were always kind to me in school. What happened?"

"You became a criminal, and I became a cop."

"Yes, well…" Crow wraps his fingers around my wrist and starts to tug me toward the door. "We'll see how you feel in a few days."

"A few days!" I exclaim, digging in my heels. "I want to go home."

"For now, this is your home," he snaps. "Get used to it."

Rather than continue fighting him, I let him lead me out of the room and upstairs. The main room where the party was is as quiet as a ghost town, making me wonder what time it is. When we reach a second set of steps, Crow stops and looks at me.

"I could easily keep you in the Nightmare Room," he says. "But I'm trusting my gut here and affording you as much freedom as I can. You'll sleep in my room and have free reign of the clubhouse while you're our *guest*, but if you try to escape, there will be consequences."

Free reign? Right. And I've got oceanfront property in Arizona to sell.

"I'm not sleeping with you," I snipe, choosing to focus on that part of his threat.

"That's another thing we're not," he snaps. "We're not rapists. And you're right. You're not sleeping with me, just in my room." Crow lowers his gaze, taking in my body, making me feel exposed despite being fully covered. "But I wouldn't be opposed to sharing my bed with you."

"Pig."

"That's you, not me."

I groan with frustration. "You're infuriating."

"And you're sexy as fuck," he counters. "Which is equally as infuriating."

He turns to continue up the steps, but he doesn't hold on to me as he walks. For a split second, I think about running, but then I remember why I came here in the first place.

Maybe Crow is doing me a favor by keeping me here. If I'm staying here and can do as I please, I'm bound to find a ton of evidence to put them all away for a very long time. If I run, I have nothing.

I lift my foot onto the first step and follow him upstairs.

A good detective does what's necessary to bring down the bad guys. And this entire situation has become necessary.

CHAPTER 9
CROW

I KNEW HER ONCE, AND I WANT TO KNOW HER AGAIN.

"THIS IS YOUR ROOM?"

I pick up the dirty clothes I tossed in the corner last night and throw them in the hamper. When I went to bed, satisfied that Addison was secure in the Nightmare Room, I didn't do it with the thought that I'd be bringing her up here today. My life would be much easier if I left her down there, but what fun could that possibly be?

"Not what you expected?"

She glances around the space as she shakes her head. "Not at all."

My king-sized bed sits against one wall, and bookshelves line another. There's a built-in desk with a mini fridge under it, and an oversized chair facing a sixty-inch flatscreen TV. I spend a lot of time here when not dealing with club business and like to be comfortable.

"There's a bathroom through that door," I tell her, pointing to one of three doors. "The tub is extra-large so if you ever want to soak, feel free."

An image of her naked beneath bubbles pops into my head, and my cock springs to life. I don't bother hiding my arousal. There's no point.

"I'll pass, thanks," she mutters.

"Suit yourself." I move to one of the other doors and open it. "Closet's in here. I'll have one of the Bangin' Betties go shopping for you. Just make a list of what you need," I say, nodding to a pen and tablet on the desk.

"Bangin' Betties?"

"C'mon, Ace, surely you can figure out what that means."

She narrows her eyes for a moment and then frowns. "And I'm supposed to believe that you're all the good guys."

"The Betties are here because they want to be here," I snap. "And they're free to leave any time they want."

"Whatever helps you sleep at night," she sasses.

I growl and close the distance between us. "Listen, you don't like me. Fine. But you will not disrespect those women. They're good girls and don't deserve your judgment."

Addison's eyes widen with shock, and she nods. "Fair enough."

I heave a sigh. "I've got some work to do. I'll have someone bring you something to eat. I'm sure you've got a killer headache from the Rohypnol so if you wanna take a nap, have at it. The sheets are clean."

I don't bother to stick around and listen to her argue. Instead, I march out of the room, leaving the door open so she knows I meant it when I said she could go anywhere within these walls.

When I reach the common room, Ghost is just walking back inside.

"He's gone, Pres," he says.

"Good. Think he'll keep his mouth shut?"

"Don't know. Kenny's a smart kid, so probably." My sergeant at arms grins. "But I put a tracker on his bike just in case. If he decides to be a douchebag, I'll take care of it."

"Thanks."

"No problem."

"Do me another favor?" I ask, meeting him in the middle of the room.

"Anything."

"Go rouse the troops. Church is in ten."

Ghost groans. "Man, you know how they all get when they're forced to get outta bed, especially after a party."

I grin. "Yeah, I know. Why do you think I'm not doing it myself?"

As I walk away, I chuckle. It pays to be the head honcho.

When I reach the meeting room, I pull my cell out of my pocket to send a quick text.

> Me: Need you to go shopping for our guest

I'm surprised when my phone pings with a reply before I can set it on the table.

> Sunny: I've got class in an hour. Can I go after that?

> Me: That's fine. Thanks

> Sunny: No problem

My brothers begin to filter into the room, one by one, each of them grumbling about the early hour. I glance at the time and realize it's only seven-thirty, but I ignore the guilt that threatens.

"We'll be quick," I promise them.

Once they're all seated, Journey calls church to order.

"I was balls deep in a nameless Playboy model," Jackyl, our club doc, complains. "What could possibly be more important than that?"

Python smacks him over the head. "You were dreaming, dickwad. It's not like you had real pussy in your bed."

"So?" Jackyl counters. "It felt very real, and that's all th—"

"Shut the hell up," I bark. "I'll make this as quick as I can, and then you can get back to your imaginary model."

"It's too late now, Pres," Jackyl grumbles. "I've gotta be at the clinic by nine."

At the mention of the free medical clinic the club owns and operates, an idea forms.

"That's perfect." I smile. "You can take Addison with you."

"Uh, dude," Journey begins. "You sure that's a good idea? I thought the entire point of kidnapping her was to keep her here?"

"Kidnapping?" Fudge asks. "When the fuck did we kidnap someone?"

"The officers voted last night," I explain. "Addison McGill came to the party with a friend of hers, both of whom were invited by Blain."

"So what?" Tracer, a patched brother, comments. "The more pussy the better, right?"

"Yeah, well, this particular chick is a detective and the daughter of Chief McGill."

"Aw, fuck," Fudge mutters. "Why the hell would Blain invite a detective?"

"Obviously, he didn't know," Poker states.

"Are we sure about that?" Screamer asks.

"Yeah," I say. "Blain isn't from around here, and he hasn't had any run-ins with the police, so he didn't know."

"Where's the bitch now?" Poker asks, his eyes narrowing.

"Her name's Addison," I snap. "And she's here so we can prove to her that we're not the evil people she and her kind think we are. She's here because I want to show her that we're also not responsible for that triple murder."

"Commit one crime to exonerate us from another." Python shakes his head. "That's risky."

"And it's already done." I lean on my outstretched arms. "I called church to fill you all in."

"Still didn't answer my question, Pres?" Poker points out. "Where is she now?"

"In the Nightmare Room," Journey says before I can reply.

"Actually, she's in my room at the moment," I admit.

Journey's head spins, and he locks eyes with me. "What?"

"Addi will be staying in my room."

"She can come to my room," Python says, his tone lascivious. "I'm more than happy to show her how I got my road name."

White-hot rage simmers just beneath my skin. "None of you will lay a finger on her," I snarl. "Addison is not here for your pleasure."

"Ahh, okay," Python drawls. "I get it. You want her all to yourself."

"That's not what I said."

"Didn't have to say it," Journey pipes in. "It's written all over your face."

I force my expression to remain neutral. "How about you quit worrying about me and my dick and focus on the fact that we have her here and need to make the most of it?"

"Back to the topic of her going to the clinic," Jackyl says. "You sure that's a good idea? What if she tries to run?"

"She won't."

"How can you be so sure?" Fudge asks.

I can't.

"I just am," I lie. "It's a win for us if she sees some

of the good we do for the community."

"If you say so," Jackyl says dryly.

A thought occurs to me. "And don't take your bike. Take the truck."

"Why?"

"Because the only bike our pres wants her on the back of is his," Ghost says with a smirk.

Ignoring his comment, I continue. "I'll pick her up around lunchtime and bring her back here. I've got Sunny going to the store to get Addi anything she might need to make her stay more comfortable. As for the rest of you, remember, she's here for a reason."

"And other than for your entertainment, what is that reason?" Poker demands.

"Watch your tone," I snarl.

"Fine. What, pray tell, is the reason that we have the lady here in our home?" he asks, sarcasm dripping from the words.

"Like I said, to prove to her that we didn't kill anyone. To show her that we're not the monsters society thinks we are." I take a deep breath. "And because maybe, just maybe, we'll end up with another ally in the department."

"Yeah, that's not gonna happen," Poker mumbles. "Remember the fight she put up when I wanted to take her gun?"

"I remember," I say. "Now, this discussion is over."

"We didn't need church for you to tell us all this," Journey states.

"You're right, we didn't. But I wanted her presence here to be official, and now it is. Also," I continue. "Kenny is no longer prospecting. He was kicked out this morning."

"What'd he do?"

"He had Rohypnol in his possession."

"Isn't that how you got Addison to stay?" Screamer asks.

"It is," I admit. "But I have no idea who he would've used it on had we not taken it. So, he's gone. Keep your eyes and ears open for any trouble resulting from his dismissal."

"Anything else?" Fudge asks.

"No. Any questions?"

"Just to be clear," Python begins. "I can't entertain myself with Addison?"

I narrow my eyes at him. "You can, but I'll cut your cock off with a butter knife if you do."

His eyes widen. "Got it. She's yours."

Addison McGill is not mine.

"She's my prisoner, that's all."

"Uh huh," Python taunts.

"Does anyone have any questions that aren't

related to sex?" I ask, turning my attention to the group as a whole.

A chorus of 'no's' fills the room.

"Good. Church dismissed."

Just as they entered, my brothers file out of the room one by one. Journey is the only brave one to hang back.

"Did you need something?" I ask him.

"You claimed her."

"I didn't."

"You did," he insists. "You don't want her on the back of Jackyl's bike, and the idea of Python getting anywhere near Addison McGill practically sends you into a tailspin."

"You have no fucking clue what you're talking about."

"And you're being stupid," he counters. When I glare at him, he holds up a hand to keep me silent. "You're not a stupid man, Crow. Not by a long shot. So why take the huge risk of keeping that woman here?"

Because I knew her once, and I want to know her again.

"I told you, it's the best way to get us out of the department's crosshairs."

Even I hear how wrong those words sound, but last night, it seemed like the best idea. And I'm not one to throw in the towel just because something is hard.

"Right." Journey shakes his head. "I hope you know what you're doing."

Me too, brother. Me too.

CHAPTER 10
ADDISON

Son of a bitch is right.

"Change into these."

I whip my head toward the door and spot a man I don't recognize. He's holding out what appears to be jeans and a long-sleeved tee, and a pair of boots are sitting on top of the meager pile in his hands.

"Who are you?" I ask, standing from the chair.

"Jackyl," he states and strides across the room to drop the clothes onto the bed. When he faces me again, he continues. "I'm the club doc, and I'm gonna be late for work if you don't hurry up."

"Why do I need to hurry so you won't be late?"

"Pres wants you to go with me." Jackyl shrugs. "And what Pres wants, Pres gets."

"He actually trusts me to leave the clubhouse with you?"

Shut up, Addi!

"Get changed. Can't very well have you looking like a hussy at the clinic." With that, he walks out of the room. "Meet me downstairs in ten!" he shouts.

Deciding to take advantage of this opportunity, I quickly grab the clothes and dart into the bathroom to change. Once I'm more comfortable, I splash water on my face and use my finger to brush my teeth.

My stomach growls, and I take that as a good sign. When I first woke up, food was the last thing on my mind.

I head downstairs looking as presentable as I'm going to get for not having time to shower. I don't know where Jackyl works, but hopefully it's nowhere too fancy.

Fancy? Not likely with this crowd.

When I reach the bottom of the stairs, Jackyl is waiting for me. He's holding two to-go cups of coffee, and he hands me one.

"I hope you like it black," he says.

"Black's fine." I take a sip of the liquid caffeine and sigh in appreciation. "Thanks."

"Let's go."

He takes long strides across the room, and I have

to quick step to keep up. Good thing I'm used to working around a lot of men.

"Where exactly are we going?" I ask once we step outside.

"I told you," he says with a hint of intolerance. "I have to go to work."

I roll my eyes. "Where do you work?"

Jackyl stops in his tracks and turns around, almost causing me to run into his chest. "Do you always ask so many questions?"

"I'm a detective, so yeah," I deadpan. "And I only asked you one question which you still haven't answered."

"This is a bad idea," he mutters.

"What's a bad idea?"

"Pres wants you to come to work with me so you can see some of the good we do," he explains. "But unless you shut the hell up, none of the work I do today will be good because I won't be able to concentrate. And I *need* to concentrate."

"Concentrate on what?"

"My patients!" Jackyl shouts. "I need to focus on my patients if I am to give them the best medical care possible."

Stunned, I watch as he turns on his heel and walks away. He stops at a truck parked at the side of the building and yanks open the door.

"Are you coming, or do I have to go tell Crow you're not cooperating?" he asks without turning around to face me.

Not ready to face Crow again, I rush to join Jackyl. We both climb into the cab of the truck, and cool air blasts from the vents when he turns the key in the ignition.

"Can I get my jacket and purse out of my car?" I ask quietly as he puts the truck in reverse.

He heaves a sigh. "Yeah." Jackyl backs the truck up and swings it around so it's facing my vehicle. "Make it quick."

I arch a brow. "You're not worried I'll just hop in my car and drive away?"

He reaches under the seat and pulls out a pistol. "Nope."

Dammit. He's calling my bluff.

Even without the pistol, I wasn't going anywhere. Not until I get what I need to take these assholes down.

Two minutes later, we're heading toward the gate of the property. I dig through my purse for some Tylenol and wash two pills down with my coffee.

"I don't suppose you know where my cell phone is?" I ask.

"I assume Crow has it."

"Of course he does."

"He's not a bad guy, ya know?"

Leaning back in the seat, I take a deep breath. "He had me drugged and kidnapped. Forgive me if I fail to see the good in him."

Jackyl remains silent for the rest of the drive. When we turn into the parking lot for the free clinic in town, I spare him a quick glance.

"You work here?"

"Yep."

"They hired a criminal?"

"First, I don't have a record," he snaps. "And second, the club owns the clinic so even if I did, it wouldn't matter."

I don't know what surprises me more: the fact that he doesn't have a record or that the club owns the clinic.

"And here I thought you knew all about us," he taunts as he parks and turns the truck off. "What happened to people being innocent until proven guilty?"

It irritates me that he has a point. The entire justice system is based on that one assumption: innocent until proven guilty. Never mind the reason I hate them so much, the reason I know they're all guilty of *something*.

A knock on the window jolts me from my

thoughts, and I twist in the seat to see Jackyl standing outside my door.

"Let's go," he calls through the window.

Are all bikers this bossy?

I climb out of the truck and follow him inside. He's greeted by several women, and he's polite but professional with each one.

"Ladies, this is Addison," Jackyl introduces. "Addison, that's Anna, Melanie, and Sandy. Sandy is the receptionist slash office manager, and the other two are my nurses."

"It's, uh, nice to meet you," I say.

"Another intern?" Sandy asks Jackyl, her tone condescending.

I stiffen at the slight, but he just chuckles. "No, not an intern. A friend. I expect you to make her feel welcome."

"Hey, aren't you a cop or something?" Anna asks.

Tell her. Ask for help.

"I am," I admit, and Jackyl cuts a sharp gaze at me. "The chief thought it would be beneficial for each of his officers and detectives to volunteer in the community, and I figured the free clinic was the perfect place."

"Oh," Melanie says. "Sort of like take your daughter to work day." Her words cut deep. I wouldn't know what that's like because my dad never took me. "But instead, it's take a cop to work day."

Before I can comment, the front door flies open, and a woman with a girl no older than five or six in her arms. The little girl is crying and holding her arm at an odd angle.

"Dr. Smith, thank God," the woman says frantically. "Chessy fell off the slide at the park, and—"

"Anna, get supplies for a cast," Jackyl orders as he gently takes Chessy from her mother. She curls into his chest, and he's careful not to jostle her arm. "Miss Dunn, go with Sandy to fill out the paperwork. Melanie and Addison, follow me."

Jackyl carries Chessy to an exam room with an X-ray machine. He sets her on the long table.

"Go ahead and lay back," he instructs. "Melanie's gonna hold your arm in place so we can take some pictures, okay?"

Chessy nods and uses her good hand to wipe away tears.

"I'll be very careful, okay, sweetie?" Melanie coos as she lifts the obviously broken limb. "We're gonna hold very still while Dr. Smith takes those pictures."

I remain in the hall and watch the scene unfold. Within these walls, Jackyl is a completely different person than he was when it was just him and me in the truck.

The rest of the morning flies by as patient after patient requires medical attention. Jackyl handles everything from Chessy's broken arm and cast to an elderly woman who suffers from diabetes. He shows each person respect and compassion, and I find myself hoping that if I ever need a doctor, he's around.

"Crow's on his way," Jackyl states when his latest patient walks out the front door.

"I'm not staying all day?"

I want to, which is odd.

"Clinic's only open until one on Sunday," he says. "And I've got other business to handle before going back to the clubhouse."

"Other business?" I ask, my curiosity getting the better of me.

"Club business." He smirks. "In other words, none of your business."

"Right. And secrets are obviously the way to get me to change my opinion of you."

Jackyl shrugs. "It has nothing to do with you and your opinion. Club business is *club* business. It's as simple as that."

"Doesn't sound so simple."

"It's simple." I whirl around at the sound of Crow's voice, and he's narrowing his eyes at me.

"Just because you want it to be complicated doesn't make it so."

"How long have you been standing there?" I ask, my eyes darting from him to Jackyl and back again.

"Long enough to know that it's going to take more than a field trip to change your mind about Soulless Kings."

Resigned to the fact that he's determined to see this through, I let my shoulders fall. "Then what's next on the agenda?"

"Lunch."

"Lunch?"

Crow nods. "Gotta eat, right?"

"And what makes you think I won't try to signal someone for help if you take me somewhere public?"

He shifts his stare to Jackyl. "Did she try to escape or tell anyone that she's not here of her own free will?"

"Nope."

Crow returns his attention to me. "That's how I know. If you wanted to get away, you'd try. Fortunately for me, you're so determined to prove your opinions of us that you'll do whatever it takes to find what you need to do that. Even if it means being held captive."

Son of a bitch is right.

CHAPTER 11
CROW

One step forward, and two steps back.

"I'm not getting on that thing."

Scowling at Addison, I grab her arm and urge her closer to my Harley. She doesn't resist, which is a step in the right direction, but she isn't eager about her movements either.

"Yeah, Ace, you are."

She looks at me incredulously. "Do you have any idea how dangerous motorcycles are? I've been at the scene of several crashes, and let me tell ya, it's not pretty."

"I'm aware," I snarl, not wanting to discuss safety with her.

"If you want me to go with you, we'll take the truck," she insists.

"The fuck we will," I snap.

"Why not? Jackyl didn't have a problem with it this morning."

"Because I wasn't about to let him take you on the back of his bike!" I take several deep breaths before continuing. "And if we take the truck now, Jackyl will have to ride my Harley home, and that's not happening. Now, get on the damn bike."

Addison stares at me for a moment as if considering whether or not arguing with me will be futile. She must realize that it is because she frowns as she throws her leg over the seat.

Once she's situated, I pull a helmet out of my saddlebag and hand it to her.

"Need help with that?" I ask.

"I got it," she bites out, and she does. For someone who claims to not like motorcycles, she seems to be a pro at strapping on the headgear.

After I climb on in front of her, Addison tries to scoot back, but I settle a hand on her thigh and shake my head.

"Stay close," I instruct. "And keep your arms around me."

She groans loudly but does as she's told. Her body heat seeps into my bones, and my dick twitches at the way she feels straddled against me.

This is gonna be a long fucking ride.

"You good with Italian food?" I ask before starting the engine.

"Yeah," she replies. "I could make a nice pot of spaghetti at my place."

I throw my head back and laugh. "Nice try, Ace."

I'm careful not to tear out of the parking lot, aware that Addison might not be used to riding. She keeps her arms firmly around my waist, and I can't help but wonder if she's simply following orders or if she wants them there.

Get your head outta your ass, Crow. She doesn't want you.

It doesn't take long to arrive at Carino's. I park on the street out front of the little mom and pop joint, then help Addison off the bike. She shakes her hair out after handing me the helmet, and grumbles about looking like crap.

"You look beautiful," I assure her.

At the look of shock on her face, I immediately want to call the words back. Instead, I plaster a smile on my face and lead her inside. A hostess I don't recognize ushers us to a table in the back, leaving us with menus.

"You can't say shit like that," Addison bites out once we're alone.

"Like what?"

"You can't tell me I'm beautiful."

"Why?"

That seems to throw her off. "Because…" She huffs out a breath. "Because I'm your hostage," she whispers.

I grin like a fool, desperate to tease her a bit. "A stunning hostage at that."

"Stop it," she gripes. "I haven't even showered today, and I'm in someone else's clothes."

"Yeah, sorry about that. You'll have stuff of your own by the time we get home. I had Sunny go shopping."

"Trace, my boy!"

Addison swivels toward the voice so fast I swear she'd have fallen off her chair if she hadn't grabbed the edge of the table.

I stand and give the older man a hug. His wife comes out of the kitchen and pushes her way in for a hug of her own.

"And who do we have here?" he asks me.

"This is Addison. Addison, these are my grandparents, Enzo and Lucia Carino."

"I, uh…" She rises from her chair to shake their hands, but they both ignore the gesture and wrap her in a hug. "It's nice to meet you both," she says when she returns to her seat.

"Trace," Grandma says. "It's been a while. We miss you."

"I know, Grandma. How about next Sunday I come over for dinner?"

"Just bring some of your friends along," Grandpa states. "I love hearing them tell stories."

I chuckle. "I'll bring Journey, Poker, and Screamer."

"And Addison," Grandpa says with a wink at her. "Bring her, too."

"Oh, I…" She shakes her head. "I don't know that I'll be available."

"Nonsense." Grandma lightly swats her with the dish towel in her hand. "You'll join us for dinner."

Addison smiles, and for the first time since she showed up at the clubhouse, it reaches her eyes. "Yes, ma'am."

"Well, we better get back to cooking," Grandpa states. "I'll bring you both out a plate of lasagna. How's that sound?"

"Perfect."

"Delicious."

Addison and I speak simultaneously which sends Grandma into giggles. When they retreat behind the swinging door, I sit back down and lock my eyes on Addison. She's staring at me as if trying to figure me out.

"What? You didn't think I had family?"

"You don't have the slightest hint of Italian in

your features, but those two," she says, nodding toward the door. "They're Italian through and through."

"My mother was adopted, and my dad, well, he was a mutt."

"Oh."

"My mother was a Bangin' Betty at the club. That's how my parents met." I watch her reactions as I talk. "Grandma and Grandpa never knew the extent of her *interactions* with the club, but they loved my dad. With both of them gone, I'm all they have left."

"How'd they die?" she asks. "Your parents."

"Mom had ovarian cancer. She died right before I started at public school." Sympathy flashes in her eyes. "Dad died a few years ago… motorcycle crash."

"Yet you still ride?"

"Absolutely. Riding is my life. And Dad's accident wasn't because he was on a motorcycle. He died because he laid his bike down to stop an enemy from hitting Fudge. He died because he was loyal."

"Wait a minute…" Addison leans forward. "Did that happen four years ago? Just on the outskirts of town to the west?"

An image of my dad lying on the pavement, bloody and broken, flashes in my mind. I wasn't there that day, but that doesn't stop my brain from forcing me to think about what he looked like.

"Yeah."

"Damn." She whistles. "That was a bad one."

"You were there?"

"Yeah. And there was nothing to indicate that there was anyone else involved besides your dad." She narrows her eyes. "Wait… there were skid marks that weren't linked to your dad's bike, but we never could tie them to anyone else."

"I know."

We clean up our own messes. Always have, always will. And it wouldn't have done a damn bit of good to have the cops trying to sort out exactly how the crash happened. It would've brought them into the orbit of our drug business, and that couldn't happen. Besides, law enforcement knowing the particulars wasn't going to bring my dad back.

"I did CPR on him until the paramedics arrived." I perk up at this bit of information, and sensing my interest, she continues. "Even managed to get a pulse for a few minutes."

"Did he say anything?"

Addison scrunches her forehead in thought. Then she snaps her fingers. "Yeah, he did. He said, 'ride or die'. He died a few seconds after that."

I bark out a laugh. "Sounds like him."

My grandpa brings our food to the table and sets the plates in front of us. "Enjoy."

"Thank you," Addison says as she takes a whiff of the steaming hot lasagna.

"Thanks, Pop."

When she takes a bite, she moans with pleasure. "This is good. Damn good."

"It is," I agree. "No one cooks better than Lucia Carino."

"I hate to admit it, but I'd have to agree with you."

After a few minutes, I decide to dig a little into her life. She's asked her questions, and turnabout is fair play.

"So, I know your dad is the Chief of Police." I smirk. "We've met on a few occasions."

"I'm sure you have."

"But what about your mom? She still around?"

Addison's relaxed manner disappears and is replaced by an icy cold shield. She calmly sets her fork down and stands.

"I'm ready to go," she says without looking at me.

"Uh, you haven't finished eating."

"And I'm not going to."

I lift my napkin and wipe my mouth before standing. After tossing down a couple of twenties to cover the tab, I reach out to guide her out of the restaurant, but she avoids my touch.

"What happened in there?" I ask when we reach my bike.

"Take me back to the clubhouse," she demands hotly.

Her eyes are bright with unshed tears, and for some strange reason, I feel like a dick. Upsetting her was not on my agenda, and that's exactly what I did.

"Okay," I mutter.

Clearly, I touched a nerve about her mom. And I was making progress too. At least, I think I was.

One step forward, and two steps back.

CHAPTER 12
ADDISON

I REFUSE TO LET THIS MAN SEE ME AT MY WORST.

"You must be Crow's girl."

I freeze just as I step inside his room and glare at the woman sitting on the edge of the bed. She's surrounded by shopping bags.

"Let's call it like it is, shall we?" I snark. "I'm his prisoner, not his girl."

The woman shrugs as if that's a tiny detail that doesn't matter. "If you were a prisoner, you'd be downstairs. I'm Sunny, by the way."

"I know."

"And you're Addison, a detective."

"I am."

Sunny wrings her hands in front of her, suddenly

nervous. "I know what you must think of me, but I'm not a slut."

Okay, not what I expected.

"I don't think that."

"It's okay, really. I mean, I do sleep with the brothers. But that's not why I stay."

"Okay," I say, drawing out the word. "Then why do you stay? Are they forcing you to?"

Sunny's eyes widen. "What? No, of course not."

"Then why?"

"Because I live here rent free," she says unapologetically. "I have a roof over my head, food on the table, and clothes on my back. All while going to school full time on the club's dime."

"You're in school?"

She nods. "For computer programming, and I've only got three semesters left. Thanks to the Soulless Kings, I'm debt-free because I didn't have to take out student loans." Sunny takes a deep breath. "And before you ask, no, they didn't make working as a club whore a condition on the money."

"Wasn't gonna ask that," I lie.

How could I not ask that? While it sounds great on the surface, Sunny is still essentially engaging in prostitution with the club.

"When I was fifteen, my parents were killed in a car accident. My aunt came down from Utah to take care of me, but she wasn't exactly *parent material*." She scrunches her nose with displeasure, and it doesn't take a genius, or a detective, to figure out why. "After a particularly bad night, I ran away. A couple of the brothers found me and brought me back to the clubhouse. They took care of me when I had no one else."

"You didn't go to the police about your aunt?"

Sunny snorts. "No offense, but the police didn't give a shit about an orphan from the wrong side of the tracks."

"I'm sorry."

And I am. I've seen great cops, and I've seen awful ones. Sounds like Sunny's only encountered the latter.

"I'm not telling you this for sympathy or an apology. I'm telling you this because I know why you're here. And I need you to know that you're wrong." She smiles sadly. "Sure, the Soulless Kings aren't perfect, but they are decent humans with an amazing capacity to give a damn about others."

I'm beginning to see that.

"I'll keep that in mind."

"That's all I ask."

Sunny moves past me to the door, but she glances over her shoulder before leaving. "You should have everything you need there," she says, nodding at the bed. "But if you need something else, let me know."

"Thank you, Sunny."

After she leaves, I start going through the shopping bags. It seems Sunny thought of everything.

Or Crow did.

There are two pairs of jeans, a week's worth of panties, two bras, seven tops, and two sets of pajamas. Factor in the three bags of toiletries and makeup, and I don't think Sunny'll have to run any more errands on my behalf.

I take the toiletries into the attached bath, along with a change of clothes, and set it all on the counter. After putting the brand-new bottles of shampoo and conditioner, as well as a razor and body wash, on the wall shelf in the shower, I turn on the water and step under the spray as soon as it's warm enough to tolerate.

I've been here for less than twenty-four hours, and I've encountered more situations that make me question my opinions of the Soulless Kings than I care to admit. As a kid, I was aware of the club. I'd hear my dad and Gary talk about them in the context of their work, but the crimes they'd discuss were always petty.

I knew Trace in school and liked him for the most part. He was a troublemaker, a class clown, but he never hurt anyone. In fact, he stood up for most kids who were being bullied.

But things changed, life happened, and hatred reared its ugly head.

"You almost done in there?"

Crow's voice startles me from my thoughts, and I shake my head to clear it. "I'll be out in a few minutes."

I quickly rinse the conditioner out of my hair and wash my body. Feeling slightly more human, I get out and dry off. Five minutes later, and with my hair wrapped in a towel, I step out of the bathroom and toss my dirty clothes into the hamper.

"Mona's called a few times," Crow says quietly from where he's sitting at his desk.

"And I'm guessing I can't call her back," I snap, not wanting to deal with him right now.

"I didn't say that."

I face him. "You're gonna let me call her?"

"Didn't say that either."

It takes everything in me not to stomp my foot in frustration. "I'm not in the mood for games," I snap. "Either I can call my friend or not."

Crow stands and closes the distance between us. My breath hitches at his nearness, and it's not out of fear.

Traitorous body.

"You can text her, but I'm going to read it, and if I suspect you're trying to tell her anything or give her some sort of distress signal, Mona will be joining you here." He arches a brow. "Understood?"

And there's the evil I knew was lurking just beneath the surface.

"Understood," I huff out.

Crow hands me my cell phone, and I quickly open the texting app.

> Me: Sorry I missed your calls. I'm fine… just hungover.

It's less than a minute before my phone pings with a notification.

> Mona: Thank God! I was getting worried.

> Me: How r u feeling? U were pretty drunk

> Mona: Hungover, same as you

> Me: Get some rest. I'll call u tomorrow

> Mona: K

"You're that confident I'm gonna let you call

her?" Crow asks from his position next to me where he was reading over my shoulder.

"Unless you want someone beating down your clubhouse door, yeah, I am." I shove my phone into the back pocket of my jeans. "Mona and I talk all the time. It'd be suspicious if I didn't call her."

"Fine."

"Speaking of tomorrow…" I lock eyes with him. "I have an early shift. Kinda gotta go to work."

"No, you don't."

"Yeah, Crow, I do. I've never missed a day, and I'm not about to start now. Besides, my dad will wonder where the hell I am and send out the cavalry."

"I've already taken care of it."

"Taken care of it how?"

"You've suddenly been struck by a nasty flu," he says with a smirk. "And the doctor told you to take the week off and rest. Even wrote you a note and everything."

"Seriously?!" I shriek. "What the fuck is wrong with you?"

"Nothing is wrong with me. I'm thorough."

"You're an ass."

Crow hangs his head as if my words hurt him. He begins to pace, doing his best to avoid looking at me at all.

"Speaking of me being an ass," he says. "What happened back at the restaurant? One minute, you were fine, and the next, you were ready to rip my head off."

"I wasn't fine," I snap. "I'm your prisoner, and that'll never be *fine*."

"Okay, whatever." He thrusts a hand through his hair. "You weren't as bitchy then."

I roll my eyes and cross the room to the bed. Exhaustion creeps in, and all I want to do is sleep.

"Answer me, Addison," Crow prods. "What happened?"

"I don't wanna talk about it."

It's true, I don't. Because if I open up that particular wound, I'll lose it. And I refuse to let this man see me at my worst.

Crow stops pacing and stands next to the bed, staring down at me. "I asked you about your mother."

I roll over, praying he'll drop it.

"What happened to your mother, Addison?"

Tears spring to my eyes, and I can't stop them from spilling over. I'd give anything to hold onto the anger, but I'm so tired, and my defenses aren't working at full power.

"Addison?"

He rests a hand on my shoulder, and that brings

my anger back in spades. I flip around and scramble to my knees. Crow tries to step back, but my fist connects with his jaw before he can get away.

"What the fuck?!" he shouts.

"You wanna know what happened to my mother?" I scream. "Fine, I'll tell you. She was murdered."

His forehead wrinkles in confusion. "Murdered?"

"Don't pretend you don't know what I'm talking about," I snarl as tears slide down my cheeks.

"But I don—"

"The Soulless Kings killed her!"

CHAPTER 13
CROW

She wants justice, to punish the guilty, but not at the expense of the innocent.

The Soulless Kings killed her!

Addison's painful scream echoes in my mind as I hold her. As soon as the words left her mouth, she collapsed. Fortunately, I was able to scoop her into my arms before she hit the floor.

I have no idea why she thinks we're responsible for her mother's death, but I intend to find out. There's no denying that my club is guilty of taking lives, but we'd never take an innocent one.

"Shhh," I soothe. "It's gonna be okay."

The fact that she's practically limp against me is a testament to the extent of her agony. If she could control her emotions, she'd no doubt be trying to kill me.

"I hate you," she mumbles.

"I know."

Her sobs continue, and they go on for so long, I begin to worry about her well-being. I reach into my pocket to grab my phone and send a text to Jackyl.

> Me: Need you in my room

> Jackyl: Not at the clubhouse

> Me: Then fucking get here!

> Jackyl: Be there in ten

Satisfied that he'll be here, I toss my cell onto the nightstand. I rub circles over her back in an effort to comfort her, but Addison's cries don't subside. Her breath hitches, her shoulders shake, and her body clenches and unclenches with tension.

"I h-h-hate y-you," she repeats weakly.

"I know."

What else is there to say? Arguing with her while she's in this state won't do me any good. Besides, I *do* know that she hates me, or at least she hates my family.

But she shouldn't. And that's exactly why I kept

her here. Because I need her to see that we're good people. We didn't do the things she thinks we did, the things we've been framed for.

If we were guilty, I'd admit to it. I don't make a habit of lying, even if it can save my own ass.

And more than that, I wouldn't lie to her. I don't think I'm capable of it.

You like her!

This isn't the first time that thought has crossed my mind. Addison McGill was the one person outside of the club who I let see the real me. Sure, it was a much younger version of me, but me all the same.

My bedroom door opens, and Jackyl strides in carrying his backpack, which I know holds some of his medical supplies. He halts when his eyes land on me and Addison on my bed.

"Pres, I'm a doctor, not a therapist," he states bluntly.

"No shit, Sherlock," I mutter. "She's been crying for a while. I'm worried."

"Last time I checked, crying isn't a death sentence."

I narrow my eyes at him. "Will you just make sure she's okay?"

Jackyl heaves a sigh. "Yeah, Pres."

While he moves closer to the bed, I shift Addison

off my lap. "Jackyl's just gonna check you over, okay?"

She sniffles and nods as she takes several deep breaths in an effort to calm herself. "I-I'm f-fine," she stutters.

Jackyl removes the blood pressure cuff from his bag and wraps it around her arm. "Are you feeling okay?" he asks, and Addison shrugs. "Blood pressure is a little high, but you're obviously upset so that doesn't concern me too much." He takes out his stethoscope and listens to her heart. "Take a few deep breaths for me." She does as instructed. "Heart sounds good." He focuses his attention on me. "She's fine, Pres. I'd say some rest would do her a world of good."

"I don't think I can sleep," Addison mumbles.

"I can give you something to help with that if you want," Jackyl states.

"Do that," I order.

"No," she blurts. "No more drugs."

"It'd just be a mild sedative," he assures her.

"You've drugged me once, and I can't remember everything that happened. I'm not about to le—"

"Oh, for fuck's sake," I snap. "He's not drugging you."

"I don't want anything," Addison insists.

Jackyl packs up his bag and moves toward the

door. "Okay. But if you change your mind, let me know."

With that, he disappears into the hallway. Once he's gone, Addison moves to the end of the bed, as far away from me as she can get without standing.

"I'd like to be alone," she says without looking at me.

I rise from the mattress. "I've got some things to do anyway."

"Like cover up a murder," she mutters with rage.

Anger rushes to the surface, and I grip her chin, forcing her to look at me. "No, Ace, I'm not going to cover anything up. But I am going to do whatever it takes to prove to you that your mother's death isn't the work of my club."

She darts her gaze away, and I remove my hand. I stomp out of the room and race downstairs to make my way to the meeting room. Again, I take out my cell, but this time, I send a text to Journey and Tracer.

> Me: Meet me in church... T, bring laptop

Three minutes later, the two of them walk into the room together.

"What's up?" Journey asks.

"We've got a problem," I blurt.

"You mean other than the pretty hostage hanging out in your room?"

I glare at Tracer, and he shrugs. "Not only does she think we killed the Limitless Throttle guys, but she also thinks the club had something to do with her mom's murder."

"Did we?"

"No." I flop down in the chair at the head of the table. "Fuck, I don't know."

Tracer sets his laptop down and opens it. "Then I guess we should find out. What can you tell me about her? The mother?"

I recall Addison's ramblings while she was crying. "She was shot during a robbery. Gas station on the edge of town."

Tracer taps his keyboard, and each click of the keys seems to stab my brain. "Here we go," he says as he flips the laptop around so Journey and I can see the screen. "Looks like she was shot with a shotgun. Cops said it was a robbery gone wrong, but the Chief is quoted as saying he believes Soulless Kings are responsible."

"Was there any evidence linking us to it?" I ask.

"Pretty sure there'd have been an arrest if there was," Journey says. "Pres, we didn't do this. We don't rob gas stations or use shotguns."

"Then why are McGill and Addison so convinced of our guilt?"

Tracer turns his screen back around and resumes tapping. A few seconds later, he grins. "Maybe this'll tell us."

Journey and I move to stand behind him and glance over his shoulder.

"You hacked the police database?"

"Did you want answers or just to speculate?" Tracer counters.

"Answers."

"Then yes, I hacked the police database."

"And?"

"You can read," he gripes.

So, I do. According to the police report, the gas station employee reported that the gunman had a Soulless Kings cut on, but his description of the patches doesn't fit. We all have rockers under our club logo that state our chapter location, but this person didn't. And the witness stated that the road name on the front of the cut was Stunner. There has never been a Stunner in our club.

"Son of a bitch!"

"We were framed," Journey says with a sigh. "It can't be a coincidence that we were set up then and are being set up now. I mean, Addison is linked to both crimes. One as a victim and the other as an investigator."

"You think she set us up?" I ask incredulously.

I might not know everything about the woman upstairs in my room, but I know enough. She wouldn't frame anyone. She wants justice, to punish the guilty, but not at the expense of the innocent.

"No, but someone linked to her did."

"But why?" Tracer asks.

"I don't know," I admit. "But I intend to find out."

CHAPTER 14
ADDISON

My motives for staying might remain the same, but I can't deny that it hasn't been so bad.

Two days later...

"Morning, Ace."

I push past Crow to get to the coffee pot. I've been doing my best to avoid him, but it's hard in such close quarters. Not to mention, we're sharing a room. Granted, he's slept on the floor, giving me the bed each night, but that hasn't gone very far in proving the club's innocence.

"Guess it's another day of the silent treatment," he mutters before walking out of the kitchen.

"Hey, Addi," Sunny greets when she walks in a second later.

"Morning," I reply.

I like Sunny. When she's not in class, she's been spending time with me so I don't get so bored. In another life, we could be good friends. But this isn't another life.

"Still not talking to Crow?" she asks after pouring coffee into her thermos.

"What's the point?"

She sighs. "I should be back from class around one. Wanna hang out after?"

"Sure."

"Okay. See ya later."

I carry my coffee out into the main room and settle on the couch. Blain and Conner are the only two around, the rest having gone to work. Over the last two days, I paid attention to everyone's routine, and the prospects seem to be unemployed at the moment because they never go anywhere unless it's an errand for the club.

"What's on the agenda today?" Conner asks when he joins me on the sofa.

"You're lookin' at it," I say.

"Someone woke up on the wrong side of the bed," he teases.

"I woke up in the wrong fucking house."

"Ya know, it occurs to me that you say that and

insist that you don't want to be here, but you've made no move to run."

He's right, I haven't because I know if I stick this out long enough, I'll get what I need to shut the Soulless Kings down for good.

But you haven't found anything yet.

"I was warned against trying to escape."

"And you're a trained cop. You could leave if you wanted."

Conner stands and moves to the bar where he sits on a stool and starts talking to Blain. I think about his words and can't help but wonder if he suspects my ulterior motive.

When I finish my coffee, I take the mug to the sink and rinse it out before putting it in the dishwasher. Then I peek through the doorway and see both men still engaged in conversation.

Now!

While there hasn't been a ton of traffic at the clubhouse since I've been here, I haven't had much of an opportunity to look around. Blain and Conner have been on me like white on rice. But now they're otherwise occupied.

I make my way down the hall toward the Bangin' Betties' room. I know Sunny is at school, and Molly and Kitty are at work. Sure that I won't get caught, I enter their shared room and am surprised to find it decorated in a very feminine style.

A search of their belongings yields nothing useful. No drugs, no weapons... not a damn thing. Next, I move to the other rooms in this hall, but the doors are locked. I'd pick the locks, but the only way I'm getting in is the fingerprint scanner on the wall.

That's not suspicious at all.

When I walk back through the main room toward the staircase, Blain and Conner don't even glance in my direction. Their conversation is animated and intense, which is great for me.

I don't need to go through Crow's room. I've already done that several times. Other than the gun and knife he had at the party, there's nothing incriminating. So, I focus on the other member's rooms.

Ghost's room boasts pictures of him and a woman who appears very frail. Jackyl's bedside table is full of condoms and lubes. And the only gun I find is of the tattoo variety in Python's closet.

If I didn't know any better, I'd say this wasn't the clubhouse of a one-percenter MC but a frat house.

"What're you doing?"

I whirl around, and my eyes widen. "Sunny."

She strides into the room and closes the door behind her. "Why are you in here?"

"I was just looking around," I say.

"Pretty sure Tracer didn't give you permission to be in here."

"I, uh…" I sigh. "You're home early."

"My second class was canceled," she says with a tilt of her head. "When Blain and Conner said I'd find you up here snooping around, I didn't believe them. I guess I should've."

"They knew?"

"Of course, they knew. It's their job to know."

"Dammit."

"I managed to convince them not to tell Crow. At least not yet."

"Not yet?"

"I told them that you'd tell him. And if you haven't by six tonight, they can."

"I'm not telling him shit."

Sunny shrugs. "Doesn't matter. He'll see it on the security cams."

"Security cams?"

Jesus, I've missed a lot.

"There's one in every public space. While they won't catch what you do in each of the bedrooms, they will show you going in and out of them."

"Shit." Settling my gaze on her, I ask, "Why are you telling me all this? Why not just turn me into Crow yourself?"

"Because I like you, Addison," she says simply.

"And despite evidence to the contrary, I'm sure you're a good detective. You'll figure out what you need to soon enough."

"You really believe in them all, don't you?"

"Yeah." She nods. "Yeah, I do."

My shoulders slump with defeat. Today isn't going to be the day I nail any of them.

"Still wanna hang out?" I ask.

"Sure." Sunny's lips tilt up into a grin. "And I've got a surprise for you."

"A surprise?"

"I already cleared it with Crow. But I need you to promise me you won't screw this up. If you do, I'll be the one to take the fall."

A knot forms in my gut. I don't like the idea that Sunny is being threatened because of me.

"I promise."

"Then let's go."

She grabs my hand and drags me out of the room. It's all I can do not to trip over my own feet as she races down the stairs, never letting go of me.

I skid to a stop when we reach the bottom and I see a familiar face across the room.

"Mona?"

My best friend turns away from Blain and smiles. "Hey, Addi," she greets.

"What are you doing here?"

"A little birdie told me you were still here." She smirks. "Why didn't you tell me you and Crow hooked up?"

Say what?!

I dart my gaze from her to Blain to Sunny and back again. "I, uh… I don't know. One-night stands aren't really my thing, and I guess I didn't want you to think less of me."

Why are you lying? Why are you playing along?

Reminding myself of the reasons I agreed to be kept at the clubhouse, I continue to lie through my teeth.

"I could never think less of you," Mona says. "You're allowed to have fun, ya know?"

"Yeah, I know, but…"

"But what?"

I take a deep breath and shake my head. "Nothing."

"I'm happy you finally let your guard down. But I am surprised you called off work." She arches a brow. "The flu, Addi? Really?"

I chuckle. "It worked, didn't it?"

"It did. I talked to your dad, and he advised me that I should stay away so I don't get whatever it is that you've got."

"So much for crack police work," Blain mutters.

It irritates me that my dad didn't give me a

second thought. He knows how much I love my job, and being sick has never stopped me from working before.

"Anyway, when Blain invited me to come back, I jumped at the chance."

Confusion washes over me. I thought Sunny brought her since she said she cleared it with Crow.

"Pres thought you might be a little bored since he had to work today," Sunny explained. "Even though Blain and Conner are on duty here, Crow agreed that she could come over as long as she wasn't a distraction to them."

That explains that.

"I'm gonna have to get back to work, but figured I'd spend my lunch break here," Mona adds.

"And I, for one, am glad she did," Blain says with a grin.

For the next forty minutes, Mona, Conner, Blain, Sunny, and I sit around one of the tables and chat while we eat. Turns out, Mona and Blain have kept in contact since the party. She seems to really like him, but I'm not convinced she's not just rebounding.

After Mona leaves, Blain and Conner home in on me.

"What?" I demand.

"You did good, Addison," Conner comments.

"She bought your act," Blain adds.

For the first time since I woke up in that horrid room on Sunday morning, it occurs to me that I'm not totally acting. My motives for staying might remain the same, but I can't deny that it hasn't been so bad.

Crow's gone out of his way to make sure I'm comfortable, and the others have done the same. Not only that, but they don't treat me like I'm a fragile flower that can't handle shit.

And even I can admit that I like that.

CHAPTER 15
CROW

Life hurts. It's brutal, but it's also beautiful.

"I'll look at it."

I lift my head and glance at Addison. She's been sitting on the bed, watching TV for the last hour, and I've been reading a mystery novel at my desk.

"At what?"

"The evidence you say will exonerate the club for my mom."

"You will?" She nods. "Why now?"

"Because I was reminded earlier that I'm a damn good cop," she explains. "And if I want to get justice, I need to know for sure that I'm actually getting it and not just putting someone away for the sake of putting someone away."

"Okay. I'll have Tracer join us in the meeting room with everything he's gathered."

I lead her downstairs, sending a text to Tracer as we go. Addison is quiet, silently following me like she's walking to her execution. In fact, it's quite the opposite. She's walking directly into the path of her freedom.

"Glad to see you've come to your senses," Tracer comments dryly, his attention squarely on Addison, when he enters the room.

"Don't be a dick," I snap, annoyed at his tone with her.

He sets his laptop down and raises his hands. "Sorry. Won't happen again."

"Make sure it doesn't."

"You know I can stand up for myself, right?" Addison chimes in.

"I know," Crow admits. "But around here, you've got back up."

"Just show me what you wanna show me," she snaps.

"Go ahead, T," I say. "Show her."

Tracer taps the keys of his laptop, then motions for Addison to stand beside him so she can see the screen.

"That's the police report from the day my mom died," she says quietly.

"Have you read it?" I ask.

Addison rolls her eyes. "Of course, I've read the damn thing."

"Then read it again."

"I know what it says, Crow," she says with her teeth clenched.

"I'm sure you do. But read it again."

She crosses her arms over her chest in a show of obstinance. "I don't wan—"

"Humor me, and read. It. Again!"

"And that's my cue to leave," Tracer states as he stands to walk out of the room.

"Why are you doing this?" Addison asks, her voice small.

"Doing what?"

"Forcing me to relive the worst day of my life."

"The last thing I want to do is hurt you." She opens her mouth to argue, but I hold a hand up to silence her. "I don't give a damn what you think, but I don't want to hurt you, Ace. What I want is to change your opinion of us, of me."

Vulnerability is not, nor has it ever been, my strong suit. But where Addison is concerned, it seems I'm willing to do pretty much whatever it takes to get my way.

She stares at me for a long moment before sitting

in Tracer's vacated chair and focusing on the police report.

"Is there anything specific I'm looking for?"

"The witness's description of the shooter."

Her lips move as she silently reads, and when she finishes, she glares at me. "How is this supposed to change my mind? Clearly one of you did it."

"No, we didn't," I insist.

"Prove it."

"I'm about to." I move to the filing cabinet and pull out the large file of emergency contacts we keep for everyone who's a club member or who resides at the clubhouse. "Look through those and tell me where you see the name Stunner," I demand as I toss the file onto the table in front of her.

It takes her a while, but she gets through each form. "Okay, fine. You don't have any record of someone who went by that name. But this is just one file, Crow. You could've hidden the evidence."

"Now look at the description of the patches, specifically the one the witness says he saw on the back of the cut that's the Soulless Kings logo."

Again, she reads through the description. "Okay, read it."

I turn so my back is to her. "Does that match the patches you see on my cut?"

Silence fills the room for several seconds before

she gasps. "Wait a second," she mutters with shock in her tone. "The witness said the logo had three skulls, but your patch only has one. And the bones that go through the skull head... The witness described those as rifles."

I whirl around and lock eyes with her. "And what does that tell you?"

"It can mean a few things."

"Like?"

"Well, for one, you could've fabricated this report," she states.

"We didn't. All you have to do is look at the web address to know it's the real deal."

"It could also mean that the witness lied. Maybe on behalf of the club."

"That didn't happen," I say simply.

"Or it means that the Soulless Kings were framed."

"That!" I bark and pound my fist on the table. "That's what it means. C'mon, Ace, don't you see? We had nothing to do with your mom's death. But clearly, whoever did, wants the world to think we're guilty."

"But..." She shakes her head in disbelief. "I don't... Who would want to do that?"

"You believe me?"

"I don't know." Addison lifts her eyes to mine,

and there's a hint of apology in them. "Who would do this?"

"The club's made a lot of enemies over the years," I admit. "But murdering the police chief's wife and pinning it on us? I have no clue who would do that."

She slowly stands and begins to pace. "I thought… My dad thought… Why?" she cries. "Why my mom?"

"I don't know."

"Even if the club didn't kill her, she died because of you."

The pain in her voice cuts through me like a hot knife through butter. I want to ease it, to take away her agony and give her nothing but good things. But that's not how life works.

Life hurts. It's brutal, but it's also beautiful.

"I'm sorry," I finally say.

"It's okay."

I grab her arm and force her to stop in front of me. Gripping her chin, I lean in close.

"It's not okay. Your pain is never okay."

CHAPTER 16
ADDISON

Punishing them for something they didn't do isn't the same as seeking justice for something they did do.

"What's wrong?"

I swivel on the stool and glance at Ghost, who sits on the stool next to me. I've been nursing my beer for a while, and up until now, everyone has kept their distance.

"Nothing."

"Bullshit."

"Excuse me?"

He grins. "I call bullshit. Something's eating at you."

"What makes you think that?"

Ghost smirks as if he's privy to some deep dark secret that he's about to reveal. "Addison, you've been here for four days now. Typically, you spend your time wandering around, snooping in any way you think you can without getting caught. When you're not snooping, you're up in Crow's room thinking about all the ways you can take the club down." He holds his hand up when I try to speak. "I'm not done. You're an only child, the daughter of a cop who thinks a woman's place is in the home, not the precinct. You so desperately want your father's approval and support that you willingly put yourself in danger to prove yourself to him." Ghost takes a deep breath before continuing. "You have a lifetime of hate which evidence now proves is misguided, yet you hang on to it like a lifeline. You're stubborn and smart, and probably one of the best detectives Marble Falls has ever seen… when the case isn't personal."

His characterization of me is spot on, and unease weighs on me. "How'd you know all that?"

"Because, Addison, like you, I was a cop," he admits. "A damn good one too."

"You seriously expect me to believe that?"

"Believe it or not." Ghost shrugs. "Doesn't matter to me."

"Then why tell me?"

"You seem very sure that the world operates in black and white," he explains. "And for a long time, I thought the same thing. Then I went undercover and met the Soulless Kings. I was introduced to the gray. I like the gray."

"That's cryptic."

"No, it's not. Let me ask you this… Do you believe that people are either good or bad? Or can they be a combination of the two?"

I think about his question for a moment. "Both, I guess."

"Exactly. And if people can be both, it stands to reason that most people operate in the gray area." He smiles as if he knows he's made his point. "Sometimes, good people do bad things for good reasons. And sometimes, bad people do good things for bad reasons. The world is complicated. The sooner you realize that, the better detective you'll be, and the more you'll understand that just because we're one percenters doesn't mean we're bad people doing good things for bad reasons. It's quite the opposite, really."

Ghost hops off the stool and stalks off across the room where he joins Crow and a few of the others. I watch them with fascination as Ghost's words sink in. He isn't treated any differently because of his previous employment. In fact, he's been made an officer. I might not know everything there is to know about MCs, but I do know that officers must be voted into their positions, and that's not gonna happen if the member isn't liked, trusted, and respected.

When I made the decision to come to the party, my intentions were noble. But now I can't help but wonder if I'm just a good person doing a bad thing for good reasons. If the Soulless Kings aren't guilty of the crimes I think they are, why am I trying so hard to find something to pin on them?

Because they do illegal shit.

And punishing them for something they didn't do isn't the same as seeking justice for something they did do.

I close my eyes and conjure an image of the police report Crow showed me. While it doesn't exonerate the Soulless Kings completely, it does cast major doubt on their guilt. But who would frame them? And why?

Bang!

Bang!

Bang!

Rapid gunfire pulls me from my thoughts, and I dive to the floor. Chaos erupts around me, but I'm not armed so I stay low. I turn my head and see Crow racing toward me and the others heading for the door, each with their own weapons drawn.

"Are you okay?" Crow demands when he squats next to me.

"I'm fine."

"Stay down un—"

"Sonofabitch!"

Crow straightens to his full height, and the color drains from his face. "What the hell?"

Unable to stand not knowing what's going on, I scramble to my feet and follow his gaze. My stomach bottoms out when I see Jackyl carrying an unconscious Sunny. Both Crow and I rush forward and follow him to the stairs.

"Ghost, Journey, and Screamer, search the property," Crow hollers over his shoulder. "Whoever did this couldn't have gotten far."

When we reach a spare room, Jackyl gently lays Sunny down on the bed. Her face is swollen and bloody, and her hair is matted with dirt. Her clothes are torn, and there's a note pinned to her shirt.

I lunge forward to grab it and read it out loud. "This is on you… Soulless Kings are responsible."

Crow yanks the piece of paper out of my hand and scans the words. "We didn't do this. We wouldn't do this." He glances at me with worry and fear in his eyes, and his pain is palpable. "Ace, ya gotta believe me. We're being—"

"Framed?" Crow nods. "Seems you get framed an awful lot."

"How could we have done this?!" he shouts. "We were all in the common room."

"Not all of you," I remind him. "And I think it's pretty convenient that she's unconscious and can't tell us who's responsible."

"If all you two are gonna do is fight, get the fuck out," Jackyl snarls as he assesses Sunny's injuries. "But if you're staying, I need help."

Crow stares at me for a moment longer, silently pleading for me to believe him, before turning away and giving his full attention to Jackyl and Sunny. While they work on her, I stay out of their way and observe.

Jackyl quickly gets an IV hooked up and starts administering fluids and pain meds. He calls out each injury as he finds them: broken arm, broken ribs, concussion. For the most part, Sunny is lucky. The bruising will fade, the breaks and concussion will heal. But the emotional trauma that follows a beating like this… that's another story.

"We got him, Pres!"

Crow glances over his shoulder and glares at Ghost, who skidded to a stop just inside the door.

"Who is it?"

Ghost lowers his gaze for a moment and takes a deep breath. When he locks eyes on Crow again, he scowls.

"Kenny."

"What?" Crow snaps.

"Screamer and Journey have him in the Nightmare Room now," Ghost states. "What's the plan?"

Crow's eyes dart from Ghost to me. "Well, Ace, care to do a little detective work?"

My eyes widen. "You want me to question him?"

Crow shrugs. "I want you to figure out why he did this? If that means asking questions, fine. If it means returning the favor to get answers, that's also fine."

"Pres, maybe that's not such a good idea," Ghost states, hesitation in his tone.

"No, it's fine," I blurt. "But I have one condition."

"Of course, you do." Crow sighs. "What's your condition?"

"Ghost assists me." When Crow arches a brow, I shrug. "He used to be a cop. What better way to get to the bottom of this than both of us going at Kenny?"

He seems to think about it for a moment before nodding. "Fine. Get started, and I'll join you when we're done here."

I turn to Ghost, who's sporting a grin that doesn't match the situation at hand.

"C'mon, partner," he says.

"Don't make me regret this."

CHAPTER 17
CROW

I JUST HOPE THIS ISN'T THE BIGGEST MISTAKE OF MY LIFE.

"She's gonna be fine."

I stalk toward the bathroom to wash my hands. It took nearly an hour for Jackyl and I to finish tending to Sunny, but she's now clean, bandaged, stitched, and sleeping. She had very brief moments of consciousness, but she was never with it long enough to confirm that Kenny did this to her.

"Maybe physically," I finally say. "But mentally? Who the fuck knows?"

"Sunny's strong. She'll get through this. We'll make sure of it."

"Yeah."

After drying my hands, I walk back into the room

and to the door. "I'm gonna go see how Ghost and Addi are doin'. You got things handled here?"

"I'm good. I'll stay with her for a while, and then get Blain and Conner to keep watch overnight and wake her every few hours."

"Okay. Let me know if you need anything."

"Will do, Pres."

Jackyl sits in the chair in the corner of the room, and I head downstairs. I'm bombarded by Kitty and Molly before my feet even touch the last step.

"How is she?" Molly asks.

"Did Kenny really do this to her?" Kitty spits out.

"She's pretty banged up, but she'll be okay," I tell them. "She's sleeping right now, but you can go up and see her if you want. Just be quiet."

The girls practically shove past me to get to their friend. I don't blame them. There's not much that could keep me away from my friends in the same situation.

I glance around the room and spot Journey near the bar.

"VP," I call out.

He spins around and meets me in the middle of the room.

"What's up?"

"They're still down there?"

"Yep."

"Have you checked in on them at all?"

He shakes his head. "Figured you'd have ordered me to if that's what you wanted."

"Okay. I'm heading down. Hopefully, they've got some answers."

"I have to say, I'm surprised you sent Addison into the Nightmare Room."

"She's a cop. Might as well put her to work for us."

Journey grins, but before he can comment on my decision further, I walk away. I don't have time to hear him analyze me or my reasons right now.

When I reach the basement, I stop to watch the monitor outside of the steel door. I'm surprised to see Kenny strung up by his wrists, his feet dangling a few inches above the floor. Addison is pacing the room, but her eyes never leave Kenny, and Ghost is leaning against the wall like he doesn't have a care in the world.

I flatten my hand on the scanner, and the door slides open.

"How's it goin' in here?" I ask as I stride inside, and the steel barrier slams closed behind me.

"Oh, just fine," Ghost replies lazily. "Your girl is damn good."

"I'm not his girl," Addison snaps. "And thank you."

"So, Ace, what answers have you gotten?"

"She's fucking crazy!" Kenny shouts. "She hit me!"

Addison stops in front of Kenny and grabs a fistful of his t-shirt. "I hit you because you hurt my friend," she seethes.

"I told you, I was paid to do it."

Wait a second...

"You honestly want me to believe this isn't just a case of retaliation for kicking you out of the club?" I ask.

"If I wanted to retaliate, I wouldn't have hurt Sunny." Kenny swings his gaze to Addison and practically growls. "I'd have hurt that bitch."

I lunge forward and yank the former prospect out of Addison's grasp and close to my face. "You lay so much as a finger on her, and I'll kill you."

Addison's sharp intake of breath barely penetrates my rage, but it does register. I loosen my grip slightly.

"I'm officially laying claim to her," I say, not thinking about the consequences of my words when I leave this room. "Put one hair on her head out of place, and there'll be a line of Soulless Kings waiting to deliver your soul to Hell."

"Uh, you're laying claim to me?" Addison asks. "I don't think so."

Kenny laughs like an idiot, and I haul my arm back before landing a punch to his jaw to shut him up.

"We can talk about this later," I tell Addison without looking at her.

Consequences… so many consequences.

Ghost pushes off the wall and steps around Kenny to stand next to me. "The one thing we haven't been able to figure out yet is who sent Kenny to do their bidding," he says, completely ignoring the tension I created in the room.

I narrow my eyes on Kenny. "Well, care to enlighten us?"

"Not particularly."

My muscles tense, and I curl my fingers into fists. "I'm not in the mood for games, motherfucker. Tell me what I want to know or meet your maker."

"You're gonna kill him?" Addison asks from behind me.

"I'm gonna subject him to the same treatment he gave Sunny," I say. "Got a problem with that?"

"I mean, I'm a cop, so yeah, kinda."

"Then get out," I snap.

"No."

I slowly turn around and advance on her. Addison takes a step back, then another and another until her back hits the wall.

"Imagine that Sunny was your daughter," I say with forced calm. "Would you want your daughter's attacker to get away with what he did?"

Her eyes dart beyond me to the swinging man but only for a moment. "Sometimes, good people do bad things for good reasons."

"What?"

"The way I see it, you've got two options." She lifts one finger. "First option is you can kill him. But then you have to live with the fact that you took away Sunny's chance to face her attacker *and* any chance you have to find out who hired him." She lifts another finger. "Second option is to have him arrested and put on trial for what he did. He'll suffer far more in prison than he will six feet under, and you'll actually have a chance to get answers."

Her words rattle around in my brain. There are pros and cons to both options, but I'm man enough to admit that there's wisdom in putting Kenny's sorry ass in jail.

"I suppose you want to make the arrest," I say, that thought giving me the most pause.

Addison sighs. "Crow, you kept me here because you wanted me to see that the Soulless Kings aren't bad. This is your chance to prove it beyond a shadow of a doubt." My heart skips a beat when she lifts a hand and cups my cheek. "You want me to trust you, and I need you to trust me."

"So, you believe we didn't kill those Limitless Throttle bastards?" I ask.

"I believe that I'll get to the truth, no matter what."

I search her eyes, trying to figure out what to do, and then I nod. "Okay."

"Okay?"

"Yeah. You're right, Ace. Trust is a two-way street. So, you can go, and you can take Kenny with you." My expression darkens. "I just hope this isn't the biggest mistake of my life."

CHAPTER 18
ADDISON

I can't let them take the fall when they did nothing wrong.

"What the hell are you doing here? I thought you had the flu."

I tighten my hold on Kenny's handcuffed wrists as I walk through the precinct toward my dad. Last night, when Crow agreed to let me take Kenny in, I honestly thought he'd change his mind. But he didn't, and I'm grateful.

Maybe he really isn't all bad.

"I did," I say. "But I'm feeling much better."

"And who do you have here?" Dad asks, nodding to the man in my grasp.

"His name's Kenny. He beat a woman almost to death." That's not entirely true, but close enough.

"Says he was hired to do it but won't give up any more information than that."

Dad stares at me for a long moment, and I half expect him to call me on my bullshit, but instead, he simply nods. "Put him in room two. We'll get to the bottom of this."

Wisely, Kenny doesn't say a word as I drag him down the hall to the interrogation room. Gary steps out of the men's bathroom as we pass it and stops in his tracks.

"Addi?"

"Hey, Gary," I greet. "Wanna help me interrogate this scumbag?"

Kenny stiffens in my hold and opens his mouth, but Gary speaks before he can.

"What'd he do?"

"Beat a woman," I say matter-of-factly. "She almost died."

I mean, Sunny could've died.

Gary's expression hardens. "Yeah, I think I'll join you."

"I want a lawyer," Kenny blurts, and Gary and I swivel our heads to stare at him. "I have the right to a lawyer, right? Those Miranda rights or whatever say so."

"Should I call the public defender's office, or do

you have another attorney in mind since, according to you, you recently came into a lot of money."

Kenny doesn't hesitate. "Get me the number to the most expensive criminal defense attorney in Marble Falls."

Seriously?

Gary heaves a sigh. "I'll get that number for him, Addi. Go ahead and have him booked for now."

Several hours later, Kenny is walking out of the precinct a free man. The entire time he was here, I thought for sure my goose was cooked. Surely, Kenny was going to throw me under the bus and blab all about the club and the Nightmare Room. But he didn't.

Why?

"You were supposed to be sick," Gary says after Kenny's gone. "How'd you end up with a perp while you were off for the week?"

"I was sick," I insist. "But all my neighbors know I'm a cop, and the woman two doors down called me saying she thought she heard screams. I went to check it out and found him attacking the lady three doors down."

Why the hell am I lying to him?

Because... something in the last few days changed for me. I know that the Soulless Kings didn't hurt Sunny, but the bone-deep hatred for the club is strong among law enforcement.

Sometimes good people do bad things for good reasons.

I can't let them take the fall when they did nothing wrong.

"Why don't we go to the hospital and get the woman's statement?" Gary asks.

Shit. Shit, shit, shit.

"I can handle that," I assure him.

"I know you can, but you're just coming off of the flu. Let me help."

Now what?

"Okay. Just give me a few minutes, and I'll be ready to roll."

"I'll meet you outside in ten."

Gary walks away, and I race to my office and close the door. After pulling out my cell to call Crow, I realize I don't have his number. Instead, I dial the next best person.

"Hey, girl, what's up?" Mona asks when she answers.

"I need Blain's number," I blurt.

She laughs. "He's mine, Addi."

"Mona, please, just give me the number. It's an emergency."

No doubt sensing my desperation, she caves.

Without so much as a thank you, I hang up and call Blain.

"Uh, who is this?" he asks after the third ring.

"Blain, it's Addison. I need to talk to Crow."

"He's not here, but I'll give you his number."

It's not lost on me that he does so, no questions asked.

"Thanks."

I disconnect the call and dial the digits he gave me.

"What's up, Ace?" Crow says with a smile in his tone.

"How'd you know it was me?"

"Because I programmed your number into my phone."

"Oh."

"So, miss me already?"

I groan. "No, I don't miss you. But we have a problem."

"Let me guess, your buddies want to interview Kenny's victim."

"Well… yeah."

"Then head to the hospital and conduct the interview."

"What? How am I supposed to do that? She's not—"

"Sunny will be there," he insists. "You've got our back, we've got yours, Ace."

My shoulders slump. "I don't understand."

"Just do your thing, detective," Crow says cheerfully. "I'll be at your place when you get home to explain."

At my place?

"O-okay."

"See ya soon."

"Yeah, soon."

CHAPTER 19
CROW

Addison might not want to admit it, but she's starting to like me.

"How'd you get in?"

I stand from the plush velvet sofa and turn to face Addison. I've been waiting for her for several hours, and seeing her immediately puts me at ease.

"Do you really wanna know?" I counter.

She slings her purse onto a hook and walks toward me. "Yeah."

I reach into my pocket and pull out a key. "Made a copy while you were still at the clubhouse."

"I should have you arrested!"

"But you won't." I tilt my head. "Will you, Ace?"

She rolls her eyes at me and stomps to the kitchen. "No, I won't. Not for this anyway." After taking two beers out of the fridge, she faces me. "Want one?"

"Sure."

I close the distance between us and take a bottle. We both lean against the counter and silently sip our brews. She's the first to break.

"Is Sunny okay?"

"She's fine. Back at the clubhouse being catered to like a damn princess."

Addison tips her head back to look me in the eyes. "You really care about her, don't you?"

"'Course I do. She's family."

"Right."

"Did the interview satisfy your cop friends?"

"Yeah. She identified Kenny, and a judge issued a warrant for his arrest. Gary and his partner are out now trying to find him."

"Gary?"

"Oh, sorry. Um, he's another detective." She smiles fondly. "He and my dad are really close. I called him Uncle Gary growing up. He's a good man."

"He's a cop."

She huffs out a humorless laugh. "Not all cops are bad, Crow. Ghost isn't."

"Ghost isn't a cop anymore."

"But he was. And as an officer of the law, I can tell

you, being a cop is more than just a profession. He might not wear a badge, but what made him a cop is still there."

"Careful, Ace. That sounds an awful lot like admiration."

Addison sets her beer down and faces me. "I guess it is."

"I think you're coming around to the dark side," I tease.

"No." She shakes her head. "I'm coming around to the right side."

"What's the difference?" I ask, genuinely interested in her answer.

"Right and wrong aren't necessarily dark and light, white and black, good or bad." Her expression turns thoughtful. "The color gray exists for a reason."

"In other words, you don't hate us anymore."

"I didn't say that."

I grin. "Didn't have to."

She pushes off the counter and returns to the living room to sit on the couch. "Can I ask you something?"

"Of course."

"How do you know when the bad thing you're doing is the right thing?"

My answer is important to her. That much is clear

by the curiosity in her eyes. I move to sit on the coffee table in front of her and lean forward.

"If I'm doing whatever I'm doing for love, family, loyalty, or protection, then I can live with the ends justifying the means," I answer honestly. "I learned a long time ago that what other people think of me doesn't matter. People are going to judge me whether I'm in leather and jeans or a three-piece suit. That's just fact." I tilt my head and study her. "Why'd you become a cop?"

"Because I wanted to follow in my dad's footsteps. I wanted to make the world a better place. Why'd you want to be a biker?"

"Same reasons, for the most part."

"For the most part?"

"Being a biker is a way of life. Riding is freedom. On the back of a motorcycle is the one place I can be one hundred percent me. It's… home."

"I get that," she says. "That's how I feel about being on the police force."

The more I'm around this woman, the more I feel like she could be home too. And that's unnerving.

Needing to change the subject, I stand and cross my arms over my chest.

"So, what happens when Kenny's arrested?"

"He'll go to jail until his trial, unless the judge sets bail. In the meantime, I'll keep working to figure out who's behind his actions. He wasn't lying about getting paid to attack Sunny. His bank accounts reflect a pretty hefty payment. But he refused to tell us who hired him."

"I'll touch base with my contact and see if they can dig up anything."

"Who is your contact?"

I shake my head. "Nope. The less you know, the better."

"Club business?"

"You got it."

Addison smirks. "I want you to know I'm going to keep investigating the murders that the club is being framed for. I'll get to the truth."

"I know."

"You do?"

"Wouldn't have agreed to let you leave if I thought otherwise."

"Right, well..." She looks over her shoulder toward the door. "I really should get some sleep. It's been a long few days."

"Then I'll leave you to it." I walk to the door and open it, but before I leave, I look back at her. "I'll be in touch."

"Surprisingly, I think I'd like that."

When I step onto her porch, it's with a grin. Addison might not want to admit it, but she's starting to like me. Which is good because I really like her.

More than I should.

As I walk to my Harley, I take my cell out of my cut and pull up a family contact to send a text.

> Me: We need to talk

> Oinker: Yeah, we do

CHAPTER 20
ADDISON

HE TRUSTS ME TO DO THE RIGHT THING, AND I TRUST HIM TO DO THE HARD THING.

One month later...

"I'M SO NERVOUS."

I squeeze Sunny's hand. We're sitting on a bench outside the courtroom waiting on the jury to render a verdict in the case against Kenny. Crow is seated on the other side of her, and there's a wall of bikers across from us. The entire club came to show their support.

"It's gonna be okay," I tell her. "Your testimony was solid. No way the jury is gonna let him walk."

"And if they do," Crow adds. "We'll handle it."

I've long since given up trying to convince him to

only operate on the legal side of things. If my short time at the clubhouse and the last few weeks have taught me anything, it's that Crow is going to do whatever it takes to keep the people he cares about safe, the law be damned.

I'm also learning that I'm not as opposed to that as I thought.

"I don't wanna hear this," I sing-song.

Crow grins. "Then don't listen, Ace."

It only takes two hours for the jury to reach a verdict so when the bailiff calls us all back into the courtroom, we enter with confidence. Rarely is a defendant found not guilty that quickly.

Once we're all seated, court is called to order, and the judge enters.

"Madam foreperson, has the jury reached a verdict?" he asks.

"We have, Your Honor."

"And how do you find the defendant?"

My stomach sinks when the woman glances at Sunny with an apologetic expression.

"Not guilty, Your Honor."

Sunny bursts into tears, and Crow shoots to his feet.

"This is bullshit," he snarls.

The judge bangs his gavel. "I suggest that

members of the gallery remain seated and quiet. I'd hate to have to charge anyone with contempt."

Crow sits but continues to mumble under his breath. I reach my arm around Sunny and rest my hand on his shoulder. His head whips to the left, and he locks eyes with me.

"Calm down," I mouth silently.

Crow narrows his eyes but gives a curt nod. He and I have talked about this, about the possibility that the justice system might fail Sunny. It's not a perfect system, after all.

And in our discussions, we kept coming back to one thing: trust. He trusts me to do the right thing, and I trust him to do the hard thing. Right or hard, Sunny's attacker will pay.

After the judge dismisses the jury, pronounces Kenny free to go, and adjourns court, Crow and I escort Sunny out into the hall. Just as we reach the door, a hand wraps around my arm, forcing me to stop in my tracks.

"You're gonna pay for this, bitch," Kenny threatens as his lawyer pulls him away from me and outside.

Crow lets out a growl, but before he can go after Kenny, I grab his hand and thread my fingers through his.

"Not here," I say with a shake of my head. "Not now."

Crow scowls as he looks over his shoulder. "Ghost, tail him," he orders.

"On it, Pres."

Ghost rushes past us, and I have no doubt he'll keep close tabs on Kenny.

"Addison," Sunny says, her voice small, like that of a child. "How could this happen? He did it. He beat me."

"I know." I squeeze her hand. "And I have no clue how it happened. Sometimes juries just get it wrong."

"But you said he confessed," she reminds me.

Which makes this all the more puzzling.

"He did."

"And twelve people still think he didn't do it?" she asks.

"C'mon, Sunny, let's get you home," Crow says, urging her through the doors. "There's no sense dwelling on what we can't change. Just know that Kenny will be dealt with. I promise."

Sunny nods and quietly lets Crow lead her to the truck parked in the courthouse parking lot. Most spots are filled with Harleys, but she's not anyone's old lady, so she doesn't get to ride on the back of one.

You were on the back of Crow's.

I shake that thought out of my head. Now is not the time to analyze my feelings for the man. Even if they are continuing to change little by little, day by day.

After getting Sunny situated in the front passenger seat, Crow walks to the tailgate, where I'm standing.

"You gonna be home later?" he asks.

I glance at my watch, which I only wear in court so I don't have to pull out my cell to check the time.

"Should be home in a few hours."

"I'm coming over."

I arch a brow. "Oh really?"

There's absolutely no annoyance in my tone. Crow coming to my house during the week has become a pretty regular thing, part of my routine. And I go to the clubhouse on the weekends. Nothing has happened between us... not that I'd mind if anything did.

Crow's actually very sweet. He always makes me feel welcome and like I belong. I don't know that I've ever really felt that before.

"Yes, really," he says. "Want me to bring a pizza or anything?"

"Nah. We can figure out food later."

"As soon as Sunny's settled back at the clubhouse, I'll head over."

"Okay. See ya there."

I return to the precinct and head straight for my dad's office. He raises his head when I enter.

"That's not a good look," he comments.

"The jury found Kenny innocent of all charges," I blurt as I flop down into the chair by his desk.

"That happens."

"But he's guilty as hell, Dad."

He leans back in his chair and steeples his fingers in front of him. "What would you like me to do about it, Addison?"

His tone sets my teeth on edge. "Nothing," I snap as I jump to my feet and whirl around to leave.

"Where are you going?" he demands.

"I came in here to talk to my dad because I'm upset," I explain. "But you can't listen, can you? You don't want me to be a cop, but you don't want me to be your daughter either."

"Sit down, Addison," he orders.

"Just… forget it."

"Sit. Down."

I glance at him over my shoulder and narrow my eyes. "Are you speaking as my father or my chief?"

"Does it matter?"

I huff out a breath and sit back down. "I'm sitting," I sass.

"When we are at work, I'm your chief, your

boss," he says. "But I'll try to be more open to listening to you as your father when you need me to."

Say what?

"I…" I swallow past the lump in my throat. "Thanks."

"Now, as for the not guilty verdict… it happens, Addison. There are going to be plenty of times throughout your career where the guilty person walks. When that happens, you have to find a way to move on, or it'll eat you alive."

I smile. "That's the first time you've acknowledged that this is my career and not just some whim."

"Yes, well, your Uncle Gary had a long talk with me, made me realize that I need to get on board unless I want to lose you."

My smile turns into a full-blown grin. "Uncle Gary's pretty smart."

Dad simply shakes his head and chuckles. "Go home, Addison. You can finish up any last-minute paperwork tomorrow."

And that's exactly what I do.

I go home and wait for Crow.

CHAPTER 21
CROW

Kissing her is like breathing, and stopping is impossible.

Addison sits on the opposite end of the couch, and she's fidgety. She has been ever since she got home from work. Despite her insisting that she's okay, I know she's not.

"Talk to me," I encourage.

"There's nothing to talk about."

"That's crap, and you know it."

She sighs deeply before twisting and pulling her leg up to tuck it beneath her. "I know I said it'd be okay back at the courthouse, but…" She shakes her head. "Crow, he's guilty."

"And he's going to pay."

"I get that, I really do. But *my* justice system failed a victim today. That's not sitting well with me."

"It shouldn't sit well with you. Hell, it shouldn't sit well with anyone. But it is what it is."

"Are you…"

"Am I what?" I ask when she doesn't finish her question.

"Are you gonna kill him?"

"Me personally, no."

"Dammit, Crow," she snaps. "Is Kenny going to be killed or not?"

"He'll be dealt with."

"You mean he'll be dead."

I don't know why she's pushing me all of a sudden. We've come to an understanding over the course of our time together. She doesn't ask too much, and I don't tell her too much. Our mutual respect allows us to have the same agenda with a very different path to get there.

"Addison, do you really want me to answer that?"

She hesitates, seemingly debating on how to respond. "Yeah, I do."

"Kenny'll be dead by the end of the day."

"Okay."

"Okay?" I arch a brow. "That's it, just okay?"

She shrugs. "Good people doing bad things for good reasons, right?"

I smile. "Yeah, something like that."

"At least Sunny can feel safe again, knowing he can't hurt her anymore." Addison sucks her bottom lip between her teeth for a moment before continuing. "We still don't know who paid him, though."

"I know. But we'll figure it out."

"And if we don't?"

I stand, grabbing her hand as I do to pull her to her feet. "C'mon, let's go for a ride. Nothing like the wind in your hair to clear your mind."

"Are you trying to distract me, Crow?"

"Absolutely," I quip. "Are you gonna let me?"

"I think I am."

Ten minutes later, Addison's changed into jeans, boots, and a hoodie, and I'm leading her outside to my Harley. I hand her the helmet, and she straps it on.

"Hold on tight, Ace," I instruct when I'm situated in front of her. "I'm not taking it slow today."

She wraps her arms around my waist and tightens her thighs against mine. My cock stirs at the contact. I've wanted her for a while now, but it's never been the right time.

Maybe today will. She needs distracting after all.

I back out of her driveway and tear off down the street. It doesn't take long to get outside of town, and once we're on a less traveled road, I open up the throttle. Addison's chest rises and falls with her laughter, and I know she's enjoying herself.

When we reach a more rural area, I slow down a little and rest my hand on the side of her thigh. Her muscles jump beneath my palm, and I smile to myself. She can pretend all she wants that she's not affected by me, but her body tells an entirely different story.

An hour passes, then two hours. I start heading back toward her place, and the closer we get, the tighter she holds onto me.

Rather than end the evening, I pull into a mostly empty lot on the edge of town and cut the engine.

"What're we doing?" she asks.

"Figured we could stretch our legs a bit."

"We're only ten minutes from my house, ya know?"

"I know." I grin. "I also know if we go back, you'll start thinking again."

"And you don't want me to think?"

I reach out to cup her cheek. Addison leans into my touch, and her body trembles.

"What's happening?" she asks, her tone raspy.

"Say the word," I whisper as I move my mouth to her ear. "And I'll stop."

She sighs, and I strike. Capturing her lips with mine, I slip my tongue past the seam and swirl it around hers. Addison moans as she throws her arms around my neck and gives as good as she gets.

I bend slightly and lift her into my arms so she can straddle my hips. We're out in the open, on full display for anyone to see, but I don't care. She's mine, and at this moment, I'm hers.

I don't know how we got here, but I know I never want to leave. Kissing her is like breathing, and stopping is impossible.

But not for her.

Addison breaks the kiss, forcing me to lower her to her feet. She rests her hands against

my chest, and I cover them with my own.

"I won't apologize for that," I say roughly.

"I don't want you to."

"I want more than just a kiss, Addison," I admit, trying like hell to keep the desperation out of my tone.

"So do I." She smiles sadly. "But not today, not under these circumstances."

"What circumstances?"

"The ones where you're trying to cheer me up. I don't want pity sex."

I bark out a laugh. "Pity sex? That's what you think it'd be?"

"It wouldn't?"

"Fuck no! When we sleep together, pity will be

the last thing on either of our minds, I promise you that."

"Oh."

"And Addison?"

"Hmm?"

"We *are* going to sleep together, and there will be zero sleeping involved."

CHAPTER 22
ADDISON

I can live with that.

"You wanted to see me?"

I lean back in my chair and look away from my computer for the first time since I arrived this morning. It's been a week since Crow kissed me, and I've been more dedicated than ever to finding out the truth of the triple murder, as well as my mom's.

"Yeah." I gesture to the chair on the other side of my desk. "I wanted to run a few things by you. Do you have an hour or so now?"

"Must be something big if you need more than a few minutes," he comments as he sits.

"It is," I confirm. "At least, I think it is."

"Okay, Addi. Hit me."

"Do you remember the witness at the gas station the night my mom was killed?"

Gary wrinkles his forehead. "The employee?" I nod. "Of course, I do. I led the investigation, so I remember pretty much everything about it."

"Right. And the guy described what the shooter was wearing," I continue. "Do you remember that?"

"Vaguely. I'd have to look at the report to really refresh my memory."

I hand him my tablet, which has the report already pulled up. "Here ya go."

Gary simply shakes his head and chuckles. "Leave it to you to be fully prepared."

"I learned from the best. Now, read the witness description and then open the photos app and look at the most recent picture."

When he's done, he levels his gaze on mine. "Okay. What exactly am I supposed to get from this."

"The description of the shooter's cut and a photo of an actual Soulless Kings MC cut don't match."

"So?"

"So, maybe they didn't do it."

Gary sits back, completely relaxed. "Addi, I know it's hard because we've never made an arrest, but they did it. They killed your mom."

"I don't think so," I insist. "Look, I've done some digging lately, and I can't find anything that points to their being a member with the name Stunner. That, along with the cut..." I throw my hands up. "That's reasonable doubt if I ever heard it."

"You and I don't have to worry about reasonable doubt. That's up to the jury."

"Since when?"

"Since always. We investigate, we gather evidence, and we present it to the district attorney. It's up to them to decide whether or not to prosecute, and then it's the jury's call if reasonable doubt factors in."

Frustrated with his line of thinking, I push. "But reasonable doubt only exists if we find it in the first place."

"And you think you've found it?"

"I know I have!"

"Where is this coming from? I know you're upset about Kenny, but that doesn't mean that there's fault to be found in every case."

"I know that. But I want to put innocent people behind bars as much as I want to let guilty people walk."

Gary leans forward. "Okay, Addi. Let's say the Soulless Kings are innocent of your mom's shooting. They were still involved in that triple homicide. So... guilty. Does it really matter what crime we get them on as long as we get them?"

"Yeah, it matters. Besides, I don't think they were involved in that either."

"What on Earth makes you think that?"

"Because I got to know them while investigating Sunny's attack." That's not the only reason, but it's all I'm comfortable sharing. "They just don't strike me as the type of people who would murder for the sake of murder."

"But they are the type of people who would murder their enemies," he counters.

He's not wrong. But he's not right, either.

"I just think we should be looking at every viable option for both unsolved cases."

"And we are." Gary stands, signaling that he's done discussing this. "Have you talked to your dad about any of this?"

"Not yet. I wanted to talk to you first since you're the lead investigator on both incidents."

"I'm gonna do you a favor and tell you to keep these thoughts to yourself. Chief hates the Soulless Kings, and he won't agree with your assumptions any more than I do."

Gary quietly pulls the door shut behind him, leaving me speechless. He's always respected my opinion. Why isn't he now?

I lift my cell off my desk and pull up Crow's contact info to send him a text.

> Me: Wanna come over later?

> Crow: Is everything okay?

> Me: Yeah, y wouldn't it be

> Crow: You've never actually asked me to come over before

> Me: LOL I'm asking now

> Crow: What time will you be home?

> Me: Leaving work early… need to get outta here

> Crow: B there in 20

Twenty-six minutes later, I pull into my garage, waving at Crow as I pass him in the driveway.

"Hey," I call to him when I step out of my car. "You can park in here if you want."

"Ashamed to have my bike seen at your house?"

"Not at all. But I think it's supposed to rain later and figured you'd want to keep it dry."

His lips tilt into a grin. "Good lookin' out, Ace."

Crow walks his Harley into the garage and puts the kickstand down when it's in the second parking spot. He closes the distance between us and presses a quick kiss to my lips like it's the most natural thing in the world.

And I don't hate it.

"Rough day?" he asks as he follows me inside.

"You could say that."

"Wanna talk about it?"

I set my purse on the kitchen counter and turn to face him. "Not really."

"Then what do you wanna do?"

"I wanna forget about it."

His grin morphs into a sly smirk. "And how do you propose I make you forget about it?"

I take a step closer to him and rest my palm on his chest. "How about that sleeping together without actually sleeping thing you mentioned last week?"

Without warning, Crow bends and lifts me off the floor to throw me over his shoulder. "Your wish is my command. Now, where's the bedroom?"

I grip the back of his shirt and hold on. "Down the hall, last door on the left," I reply with a laugh.

Crow carries me like a man with a purpose. The dark gray plush carpet of my bedroom comes into view and seconds later, he tosses me onto the mattress.

"Take your clothes off," he orders, his tone gravelly.

He begins to strip, dropping one item of clothing

on the floor after another. I miss most of the show because I'm scrambling just as fast to get naked.

"Fucking hell, you're gorgeous," he says as he climbs on top of me and straddles my hips.

His cock brushes my inner thigh, and I shiver at the contact. There's not going to be anything slow about us coming together today. It's gonna be hot, fast, and primal.

Exactly what I need right now.

"Gimme everything you got, Crow," I demand. "We can do nice and slow later."

"Yes, ma'am."

Crow reaches between us and guides his dick to my core. My hips buck when he enters me, and I dig my fingers into his ass cheeks to hold him close.

"You're killin' me," he groans.

"Don't feel dead to me."

Crow begins to slide out until just the tip remains, and then he impales himself again. Over and over, he fucks me, until my mind is full of nothing but numbing pleasure. He circles his hips, putting pressure on my clit, and I match him thrust for thrust.

"C'mon, Addi, come for me."

"I…" I throw my head back as my body begins to quiver, and the words are lost forever.

Crow's body stiffens, and his cock pulses with his

release. My pussy clamps around him, taking his pleasure as my own rips through me.

He collapses on top of me and rolls to the side, tucking me against him as he goes.

"I've wanted to do that since the moment I laid eyes on you."

"I was nine," I deadpan.

Pushing to his elbow, he stares down at me with wide eyes. "You remember that?"

"I remember Ms. Cochran forcing me to hang out with the new boy in class," I tease. "I was so mad at my dad that day, but somehow you made me forget." I duck my head. "You made me forget then, and you made me forget now."

Crow grips my chin and tips it up before leaning close to my ear.

"I'll always make you forget," he whispers.

"Just a good guy doing bad things for a good reason?"

"Just a normal man doing incredible things to an amazing woman for all the right reasons."

"I can live with that."

CHAPTER 23
CROW

Son. Of. A. Fucking. Bitch!

"I'm surprised you made it."

I climb off my Harley and glare at Journey. We've had this meeting set for a few days, and nothing was going to keep me away. Not even a naked Addison begging me to stay in bed with her.

"Wouldn't miss it."

"You know you're wearing the same clothes you had on yesterday," my VP comments, his tone conversational.

"I know."

"And why are you wearing the same—"

"I stayed at Addison's place last night," I snap. "Now can we focus on the business at hand and gossip like schoolgirls later?"

"Sure, whatever you want, Pres."

"Don't be such a smart ass."

I stride away from him to enter the little dive bar where we agreed to meet the new President and Vice President of Limitless Throttle. It's farther away than I'd like to be, but it's better than the warehouse. It took some convincing on their part, but I finally chose to give them the benefit of the doubt that they really believe we had nothing to do with the deaths of their brothers.

"There they are," Journey says and leads the way to the booth in the back corner.

"Glad you could make it," one of them says as we sit across from them. "I'm Shuffle, the new Pres. And this is Bear, my VP."

"I'm Crow, and this is Journey," I reply, pointing to my brother.

"As I said on the phone, we know your club didn't have anything to do with killing Snap, Trick, and Forge," Shuffle explains. "Snap was smart enough to have men posted outside for that meeting, and they all reported seeing a single white male enter the warehouse and leave with blood on his clothes before you even arrived."

"I'm guessing none of them told that to the cops because we're still considered suspects," Journey snaps.

"Actually, they did. The detective took their statements, and we assumed that would be the end of it. I'm sorry that hasn't been the case."

"We don't need your apology. We need the record set straight."

"And we'll do whatever we can to help with that." Shuffle leans forward, resting his elbows on the table. "Rival or not, we don't condone putting men behind bars for crimes they didn't commit."

"Right," I drawl. "And I'm supposed to believe you've got nothing but well wishes for us?"

"Look, we'd love nothing more than to run the Soulless Kings out of Marble Falls and be the only game in town," Bear admits. "But after a lot of discussion amongst our brothers, we feel like our clubs working together would be much more mutually beneficial."

"More financially lucrative, you mean," Journey states.

Shuffle shrugs. "Either way, we both win."

"What are you proposing?" I ask.

"We'd like to take the gun business out of your hands, and if you agree to that, we'll stay out of the drug trade."

Journey and I exchange a look. We've also discussed our rival at length as a club, and came up with a few proposals of our own.

"You open to a counteroffer?" I ask.

"Depends."

"We still maintain our position as the leading supplier for both guns and drugs, and Limitless Throttle handles all distribution," Journey proposes. "Because you'll be the ones on the streets taking the day-to-day risk, we'll cut you in at forty percent of the profits."

Shuffle raises a brow skeptically. "That's quite a bit higher than the standard profit share."

"It is."

"Does that offer have anything to do with the woman in your life, Crow?"

It shouldn't surprise me that they know about Addison, but if they think they can use her against me, they've got another thing comin'.

"Leave her outta this," I snarl. "Mention her name again, and we take our offer elsewhere."

Shuffle lifts his hands in surrender. "I meant no disrespect, really. But I know for a fact that you weren't anywhere close to willing to make that kinda deal with my predecessor. Makes a man wonder, is all."

"Wonder all you want, but Addison isn't fair game." I lean forward and clasp my hands on the table. "In fact, if we're going to make a partnership like this work, then I stipulate that no violence is to take place between the two clubs unless war is declared by the presidents."

Now it's Shuffle and Bear's turn to exchange a look. When they return their attention to me, they both nod.

"Agreed."

"Good." I extend my hand, and Shuffle shakes it. Journey and Bear do the same. "Now, before we go, I want the description of the man seen at the warehouse that day. I'll take it to my contact and see if he'll get things going in the right direction."

"Like I said, it was a white male," Shuffle begins. "Approximately six foot one, late fifties, rumpled suit and tie…" He glances at Bear. "Anything else?"

"When he opened the door, one of our men swore he saw a tattoo on his forearm. He also had dress shoes on, but they weren't the expensive kind. Definitely department store quality and very worn."

Son. Of. A. Fucking. Bitch!

CHAPTER 24
ADDISON

All of my training slips away, and fear like I've never felt rises to the surface.

"Get your gear, and let's go."

I quickly jump to my feet and rush around my desk, snagging my badge and gun as I go.

"Where are we headed, Gary?"

"I've been doing some thinking since we talked yesterday, and I decided to reach back out to that witness. He's agreed to talk to us, but he's only got a short window of free time today."

"Seriously? You believe me then?"

"I don't know what I believe other than it warrants another interview," he says.

Not one to look a gift horse in the mouth, I quietly follow him out to the squad car.

"Does my dad know about this interview?" I ask once we pull out of the parking lot.

"No, Addi," he admits. "I didn't want to tell him until I actually had more information to give him. Don't want to get his hopes up, ya know?"

"Makes sense." I watch our surroundings as he heads west. "Where are we meeting this guy?"

"His house."

"Okay."

The further away from the precinct we get, the more hopeful I become. Is today the day I finally prove who killed my mom? Or at least, who didn't?

My cell vibrates in my pocket, and I pull it out to see who's calling. Crow's name flashes on the screen. I tap the side button to stop the vibrations and make a mental note to call him back later.

When Gary turns on Corner Street, a thought niggles at my brain.

"Did the witness move?"

"No, why?"

"Because I studied that file, and I could've sworn he lived on Torrence Ave," I explain.

"So?"

"Wouldn't it have been quicker to stay on Fir—"

"Jesus, shut up!" he shouts, shocking me into silence. "Why couldn't you just keep your nose out of shit?"

"What are you talking about? Gary, what's going on?"

"You couldn't let sleeping dogs lie, could you?"

"I don't know wha—"

"I had things handled," he continues as if I hadn't even spoken. "A few unsolved cases weren't going to hurt the department, and I was making bank so I could retire early." His cell phone rings, and he yanks it out of his suit jacket pocket to glare at the screen. "Leave me the fuck alone!"

"Who, Gary?"

"Ya know, I knew you didn't have the flu," he says casually. "I knew Crow and his brothers were keeping you at the clubhouse."

"But how?"

"I've served numerous search warrants at that place." He chuckles, but there's little humor in the sound. "It's funny… I never find anything worth taking, but I always manage to leave a little something behind."

"Bugs, Gary? Did you bug the clubhouse?"

"Of course, I did. I couldn't very well work with them and not know exactly what's going on behind my back."

So many thoughts swirl around, so many questions. But I have no clue where to start or what to say. Wrapping my head around the fact that this man isn't at all who I thought he was is going to take more than a few minutes.

Does my dad know?

"Where are you taking me, Gary?" I ask, trying to distract him so I can send a nine one one text to Crow.

It doesn't work. Gary whips his duty weapon out and points it at my head. "Throw that out the window," he orders. "Now!"

Groaning, I do as I'm told. I have no desire to die today.

"Where are you taking me?" I repeat.

"Somewhere you won't be found."

That thought isn't at all comforting, but then he turns on Baker Road. Suddenly, I know where we're headed.

"You really think they won't find me at your house, Gary?"

"Shut up."

"C'mon, Gary. Be smart about this," I cajole. "I'm the police chief's daughter. This isn't going to go away. My dad will never stop looking."

As long as he's not dirty, too.

"Yeah, he will," he insists. "I got him to stop looking into your mom's death, didn't I?"

A thought hits me like a freight train, and bile rushes up the back of my throat.

"I'd have gotten away with it. Hell, I *have* gotten away with it so far."

I'm afraid to ask, somehow already knowing the answer, but I don't let that stop me.

"Gotten away with what?"

"I could've sworn I had the patches right," he mutters. "A few minor details, and all I've done comes crashing down."

"You killed her, d-didn't you?"

"Yes!" he screams maniacally. "I killed her. I killed her and those fucking bikers at that warehouse. And I'm gonna kill you next."

All of my training slips away, and fear like I've never felt rises to the surface. This crazy man is really gonna kill me.

CHAPTER 25
CROW

Crazy is crazy, and sometimes, crazy is also smart.

"She still not answering?"

Journey and I have been standing in the dive bar parking lot since the moment I realized the Limitless Throttle brothers saw my law enforcement contact at that warehouse.

I shake my head. "No, and neither is Gary."

"Try her again," he says. "I'll call Tracer and get him working on tracking her down."

Addison's phone goes straight to voicemail this time. I also tried calling her at work but was told she was out in the field and wouldn't be back in the office until tomorrow.

I dial Gary's number and press the speakerphone icon. It rings six times, and finally, he picks up.

"What the fuck do you want?" he barks.

So, this is how he wants to play this.

"Gary, where's Addison?"

"She's at work."

"No, she's not," I seethe. "I've called the precinct and her cell… can't get a hold of her."

"I don't know wh—"

"Cut the bullshit," I snap. "Tell me where she is, and maybe I decide to let you live to see another day."

"Crow, is that you?!"

Addison's voice sends relief straight through me. But it's short-lived when the unmistakable sound of a slap and my woman crying out in pain seeps through the line.

"I swear to Christ, Gary, if you hurt her…"

"What?" he counters. "What will you do if I hurt her?"

"I'll gut you like you gutted those three guys. The difference is, I won't leave a body for anyone to find."

Journey disconnects his call with Tracer and mouths, "He's on it."

I nod.

"What will it take to make this all go away?" Journey asks.

"I get the pres and vice pres… I'm flattered."

"Gary," I snarl.

"Okay, you want this to end, here's what I want." He takes a deep breath. "I want one of your boys to confess to killing Mrs. McGill, and another to confess to the triple homicide. I also want a million dollars wired into my account by midnight so I can retire and move to a beach somewhere."

"See, that's not gonna happen," I tell him calmly.

"Then Addison is gonna meet the same fate as her mommy."

The call is disconnected, and I throw my head back and let out an agonizing scream.

"Bro," Journey says, resting a hand on my shoulder. "We're gonna get her. She'll be fine."

"He hit her, man. I heard him hit her."

"And she's not some wimpy broad. She'll be okay."

Journey's phone rings, and he answers it right away.

"Please tell me you've got something," I beg when I see that it's Tracer.

"Her phone isn't active right now, but the last known location was about a mile away from Baker Road which is where—"

"Gary lives," I finish for him. "He's taking her to his house."

"Idiot," Journey gripes.

"Tracer, J and I are headed for them. Tell Jackyl to be on standby in case medical attention is necessary."

"You got it. Go get your girl, Pres."

My girl.

Addison and I have spent so much time together, even finally slept together, but we've never put a label on what's between us. I think it's about time that changes.

Journey and I tear out of the parking lot and ride as fast as our Harleys will allow. Fortunately, I know a route to Gary's place that doesn't require us to go through any towns so hopefully, we don't run into traffic.

While I ride, I rack my brain for any signals I missed about Gary being off his rocker. It brings me no comfort to realize there were no signals. Crazy is crazy, and sometimes, crazy is also smart.

But he's not quite as smart as he believes if he thinks I don't know where he lives. The second he was added to the club's payroll, a dossier on him was created with every detail Tracer could gather.

Two and a half hours later, Journey and I are pulling off to the side of the road about half a mile from Gary's house.

"We'll walk the rest of the way," I say as I check my weapons.

"I'll follow you."

I'm coming, Addison. Just a few more minutes.

CHAPTER 26
ADDISON

I'd bet my life on it.

"I TOLD YOU THEY WEREN'T COMING."

Gary paces the length of the hidden room in his basement. I spent hours upon hours in this house growing up and never even knew he had a basement, let alone a secret kidnapper's lair.

"Then you don't know them very well," I snarl.

"It's been hours, Addi," he reminds me. "If they were coming, they'd have been here by now."

Gary doesn't know what I know. Crow had a meeting a few hours away so it's going to take him time. But he'll be here. I'd bet my life on it.

You are betting your life on it.

"Years ago, when I had that cage built," he says, nodding to the steel bars surrounding me. "I really didn't think I'd ever need it. But I knew I had to have a backup plan, just in case."

"Back up plan for what?"

Keep him talking.

"Framing a one-percenter club takes planning, precision." There's pride in his tone, more pride than I've ever heard him muster about a case. "But I wanted money, and they had that in spades from all the drugs and guns they run." He stops next to the lock and wraps his fingers around two of the bars. "Create problems for the club so they'd have no choice but to seek out someone on the inside. Make myself available to be that someone. Demand money. Create problems, make myself available, demand money. Wash, rinse, repeat. Wash, rinse, repeat. Follow my own checklist and become a rich man. It was easy, Addison," he says with a sigh. "Until you came along."

"What did I have to do with any of it?"

"You ask questions, you dig and dig and dig until there's no dirt left to cover my tracks."

"In other words, I'm good at my job." Sarcasm drips from my tone, and I yank against the handcuffs linking me to a bar.

Gary begins to pace again. "It's ironic really."

"What is?"

"Your dad tried so hard to keep you out of law

enforcement, and the entire time, I played the role of the supportive family friend. Maybe if I hadn't, you'd have chosen another career path, and I'd be free of all this bullshit."

"It wouldn't have mattered if you were supportive or not," I bite out.

"I guess we'll never know, will we?"

"Guess not."

Gary gets quiet but continues to pace. Every few minutes, he slows in front of a bank of monitors and stares at them.

"Well, well, well," he says sometime later. "I guess you were right."

"About?"

"We've got guests."

Crow!

"Don't move, Addi," he commands cheerfully. "I'll be right back."

With that, he closes the door that barricades this room from the rest of the space. Darkness surrounds me, as does an eerie silence. I strain to listen for any sound to indicate that Crow is here for me.

But there's nothing.

I start pulling on the handcuffs, doing anything I can to loosen them, to get free. I struggle so hard that I feel a thick liquid dribble from my wrists.

The scent of copper fills my nostrils, and for a

moment, I worry that I'm losing too much blood. I manage to calm myself down and recognize that my senses are heightened due to my sight being non-existent.

I have no idea how much time passes, but light filters into the space when the door bangs open.

"Addi!"

"Crow!"

CHAPTER 27
CROW

There isn't a damn thing that could make me give her up.

Seven minutes earlier...

"You take the front, and I'll take the back."

Journey strolls up the sidewalk to Gary's front porch as if he's a long-lost relative who just came for a visit. I make my way to the back, and I'm not nearly as sly. I couldn't care less if we're caught. As long as I walk away from this with Addison on my arm, the rest can be figured out.

"Ready?" Journey's voice comes through the coms.

I've never been more grateful that we always keep some in our saddlebags, just in case.

"On my count. One, two, three."

I kick in the door and rush inside. Two seconds later, Journey comes racing through the front door, having quickly picked the lock. We go from one room to the next, clearing them as fast as we can.

As we finish with the first floor, we move to the staircase, but Gary's voice has us both whirling around.

"She said you'd come," he says casually. "I didn't believe her."

"Because you underestimate her," I snap. "You shouldn't do that."

Journey has his gun trained on Gary, and I lower mine in an effort to lull him into a false sense of security. And Gary, the fucking pissant, has his gun pointed directly at my chest.

"I told you what I want," Gary begins. "That's what it'll take to get her."

"No, it won't."

I expect him to argue, to make more demands, so the searing pain that tears through my thigh when he pulls the trigger knocks me to my knees. Journey fires in response, but he does as he's dropping to my side, and the bullet goes wide.

"If you think that's bad, you should see what I did to Addi," Gary taunts.

"Is it anything like what you had Kenny do to Sunny?" Journey asks as he helps me to my feet.

"Figured that out, did ya?"

"Wasn't too much of a leap once we realized you're a corrupt bastard." I take a deep breath and force the agony in my leg to take a back seat to my rage. "I'm sure you paid off the jury or something. That's the only way he was able to walk outta that courtroom."

"And now he gets to live a long, happy life, while the rest of you, well, don't."

I throw my head back and laugh.

"What's so funny?" Gary demands.

"The fact that you think Kenny's heart is still beating," Journey replies. "He was dead within an hour of leaving the courthouse."

"Yet another murder the Soulless Kings are gonna go down for."

"We know how to get rid of a body, Gary," I say, my tone calm, cold. "Now, tell me where Addison is so we don't have to get rid of yours."

And like every criminal who's ever walked the planet, Gary thinks he's smarter than everyone else.

"She's downstairs, caged up like an animal."

"Go," Journey says. "I got this."

I lunge forward at the same time Journey pulls his

trigger. Gary falls to the floor just as I pass him. When I cleared the kitchen, I noticed a door but thought it was the pantry. It has to lead to the basement because it's the only door unaccounted for on the first floor.

Yanking open the door, I shout for Addison. There's no response, and my stomach flip-flops. When I reach the bottom of the stairs, I turn in circles to survey the space. There's nothing down here. It's all concrete and—

There! A tiny speck of something shiny on the wall catches my attention. I cross to it and realize it's a button. I press it and step back as the concrete wall pops out and slides to the right, creating an opening.

"Addi!"

"Crow!"

I run toward the sound of her voice, my path barely lit by the light that filters through the opening.

My blood boils at the site of her in a cage. I focus my attention on the lock and start to work at picking it.

"Where's Gary?" she asks, panic in her tone. "He went upstairs and—"

"He's still up there. Journey's got him."

It takes me longer than I'd like to open the gate and step inside with her.

"I'm handcuffed too," she says.

"Not for long."

Far less time passes as I undo the cuffs. It's not the first time I've picked a set, and I doubt it'll be the last.

"You're bleeding," Addison says, throwing her arms around my neck when she's free.

"So are you," I reply, referring to her wrists.

I gently ease her back and lock eyes with her. "He hit you."

"He did. But I'm okay."

"Did he do anything else to you?"

Addison shakes her head. "Nothing other than rant and rave about all the shit he's done over the years. All for money, Crow. He did it all for money."

I cup her cheeks and press a kiss to her lips. "Your mom?"

Pain flashes in her beautiful irises as she nods.

"I'm so sorry, Ace."

"At least the truth is out."

"Doesn't shrink the hole in your life because she's gone though."

"No, it doesn't."

I help her to her feet before lifting her in my arms.

"Put me down," she protests. "You're hurt too."

"I'm fine. It's a flesh wound."

"It's a gunshot wound."

"How'd you know? Did you hear the shot?"

"You don't call me Ace for nothing."

Her teasing manner fills my heart with happiness. If she's being sassy, she's going to be okay.

"Crow?"

"Yeah?"

"Did you kill him?"

I carry her up the stairs without responding. Journey has Gary pinned to the floor, a boot in his chest, and a gunshot wound in his stomach.

"You didn't," she breathes when she spots him.

"I couldn't."

"Why?"

"Despite what he's done, he was a major part of your life," I explain. "It's not up to me whether he lives or dies."

What I don't say is good ol' Gary is gonna die. One way or another, I'll get him.

"Put me down," she orders softly.

I set Addison on her feet, and she sways slightly. After making sure she's steady, I keep a hand on her arm while she closes the distance between her and her enemy.

Before I know what's happening, Addison reaches for Journey's gun, aims it at Gary's head, and pulls the trigger.

"That's for killing my mom, you fucking piece of shit."

The gun falls to the floor, and she steps over the

corpse of a man who she thought she knew and walks right out the front door.

Journey grins. "Please tell me you're keeping her, Crow. I'm begging you… keep that woman."

"There isn't a damn thing that could make me give her up."

EPILOGUE

ADDISON

YOU KIDNAPPED ME, YA BIG OAF.

Six months later...

"I'M PROUD OF YOU, ADDISON."

Tears spring to my eyes as my father wraps his arms around me. I was awarded a medal of honor for everything that went down with Gary, and the ceremony just ended. Other than me, Crow and Journey are the only two people who know how he really died. The official story is that I had to kill him in self-defense.

There was a time when I would've hated that there were two different versions, but that time is long gone.

"Thanks, Chief," I whisper into his neck.

My Dad still struggles with the betrayal of his best friend, and I'm not sure it's something he'll ever totally recover from, but we have each other, and we'll get through it together.

"I thought Crow was going to be here," he says when he steps back.

I swivel my head to search the crowd and spot Crow, along with several Soulless Kings, standing at the back of the room.

"How could you miss that?" I ask, nodding toward the group.

"I should've known they'd all be here to support you."

One positive thing that came out of Gary's crazy is that my dad now knows the real culprit behind who killed his wife. Having all the information allowed him to open his mind to the possibility that the club isn't as bad as he thought.

Sure, he doesn't know they still have their hands in illegal dealings, but what he doesn't know can't hurt him. Crow and I make sure of that.

"Go, be with him," Dad says, gently shoving me in that direction.

"You're still coming for dinner tonight, right?"

"Are Lucia and Enzo cooking?"

There's been numerous family dinners at the Carino's house over the last few months. Those nights are one of the things that helped bring my dad around as far as Crow is concerned.

"You know they are," I tease. "It wouldn't be a celebration if they weren't."

"Then I'm still coming. Seven, right?"

"Yep. But you can come earlier if you want."

I watch as my Dad walks away, shaking the hands of other cops as he weaves through the crowd. He beams at them when they congratulate him on such a 'fine daughter', and it warms my heart.

"Hey, Ace."

I smile and turn on my heel at the sound of Crow's voice. "Hey."

"Congrats, Addi," Journey says and wraps me in a hug. "Proud of you."

"We all are," Ghost adds when he takes Journey's place.

"You're my hero," Sunny jokes.

"Would you all get your damn hands off my woman?" Crow snaps.

He pushes them out of the way playfully and grabs my hand to yank me into his chest.

"You're amazing," he tells me.

I wrap my arms around his waist. "So are you."

"I don't know what I did to deserve you, but whatever it was, I'm grateful."

I tip my head back and smirk. "You kidnapped me, ya big oaf."

He glances around the room. "Shh. I don't wanna be arrested."

Crow

I'm in this forever, Addison.

"CAN WE TALK?"

I shift so I'm sitting up and leaning against the headboard. Addison's leg is draped over my thighs, and her expression is more serious than I'm used to after having sex.

"It's never good when those words come out of a woman's mouth."

She rolls her eyes. "Can we talk or not?"

Nerves rattle me, but I nod. "Sure."

"You know I'm never gonna give up my job, right?"

"And I'd never ask you to."

"Will that work?"

"What?"

"A cop and a biker… can that work?"

"It's been working the last six months, hasn't it?" I counter. "Or am I missing something?"

"It's been working, but we've never really discussed how it would work long-term if we stayed together."

"Do you want to stay together?"

"Can it work?"

"Answer my question first."

'But I asked you first."

"Dammit, Ace, just answer me."

She huffs out a breath. "Yeah, I want it to work. I love you, Crow. And I know you love me."

"If we want it, it can work. We'll make it work."

"We shouldn't have to force it."

"Have you felt like you've had to force anything?"

"No."

"Then, I repeat, it can work."

"Are you in this for the long haul?" she asks, lowering her gaze as if she's afraid of the answer.

I grip her chin and lift, staring into her eyes. "I'm in this forever, Addison."

"Are you in this to the point where you'd move in with me?"

I can't help but chuckle. "You think I wanna live apart for the rest of our lives?"

"No." She shakes her head. "But…"

"Spit it out," I growl.

"I think you should move in here."

"You don't want to live at the clubhouse?"

It's not a question I need to ask, but I want her to know she can tell me. I'm not a stupid man. A detective shacking up with an entire one-percenter club is bad optics. And I'm not about to make her look bad. She's too good for that and deserves better.

"It's not that I don't want to," she hedges.

"Yeah, we're not living at the clubhouse," I say, having no desire to make her squirm. At least not until she's ready for round two.

"You're okay with that?"

"As long as you understand that there will be times that I'm needed there or nights we might have to stay there. I'll keep it as limited as I can, but that club is as much a part of me as being a cop is a part of you."

"I can live with that."

"Then I can live here."

She grins. "When?"

"When what?"

"When can you move in?"

"Is tomorrow too soon?"

"Tomorrow can't come fast enough."

NEXT IN SOULLESS KINGS MC: MARBLE FALLS, TX

BOOK 2: JOURNEY

Coming soon!

IF YOU HAVEN'T READ THE ORIGINAL SOULLESS KINGS MC SERIES:

START WITH BOOK 1: FENDER

Fender...

One night. That's all it takes for a person's life to forever be changed. One chaotic, unexpected, inevitable night and hundreds of bullets, two of them hitting my parents. I was born to be a Soulless King, born with sworn enemies and a loyal streak. Like a phoenix, I rise from the ash and vow to bring hell upon those responsible.

The problem with my vow is I'm not sure who is to blame. They tell me it's the temptress with emerald eyes, the one who used to share my bed. How can I be sure since she left without giving me the chance to find out the truth?

Now that she's back, she won't get away before I ask my questions. But what if I don't like the answers?

Charlie...

As the princess of the Black Savages, I was raised to believe one thing: my club is my family, no matter what. But when they are responsible for shattering the life I created, I do the only thing I can. I run.

The thing about running is I can't do it forever. Life, past transgressions, tragedy… they hunt me down and drag me back, shoving me into the deep end of fate. And fate is a fickle bitch.

What if my fate is with *him*, the president of the Black Savages' sworn enemy?

PROLOGUE

They say your life flashes before your eyes at the moment just before death. They fucking lied.
Fender

Slick.

Wet.

Hot.

Perfect.

That's the only way to describe the pussy I'm buried in. Charlie moans and the sound seems to echo around us in flawless rhythm with the headboard banging against the wall.

"That's it, baby," I growl as I reach between our bodies and rub circles over her clit with my thumb.

Charlie's eyes resemble an emerald in its purest form, and I'm lost, drowning in a sea of green. They widen and her pupils dilate the second her orgasm begins. Tingles race down my spine, and my body tenses as I join her.

We explode together, and the sounds we've created die down. My heart is pounding, and her breathing is labored. I roll off of her, carrying her with me and tucking her into my side.

"Holy shit, Fender."

"What?" I ask, a grin tugging at my lips. She always says the same thing after we fuck. Always.

"It gets better every—"

"Fender, get the fuck out here!"

The pounding on my door and the urgency in Piston's voice has me springing from the bed and grabbing my gun from the nightstand. That's when it registers. Gunshots, yelling, glass shattering.

"Fender! Now!" Piston's fist is an inch away from my face when I throw open the door. "Black Savages stormed the club. Get dressed and c'mon!"

I glance over my shoulder and see Charlie shoving her legs into her jeans. Her ass is encased in the black lace I pulled off her body with my teeth not a half hour ago. I hate to see her cover her flesh, but I can't think about that right now.

"Get in the fuckin' closet and don't come out. Not

for anything." I grip her bicep and drag her to the door in the corner of the room, throw it open and shove her in.

"Maybe I can talk to them. Maybe I—"

"No. They're past talking and so am I." I crush her lips in a bruising kiss before shutting the door in her face.

I dress as quickly as I can and mentally prepare for what I'm about to face. Certainly nothing good. I make my way down the hall, my gun cocked and ready to blow away any Savage that gets in my path.

I just pray it's not Dyno. It would be great to take out the president of the Black Savages, but I can't do that to Charlie. I can't kill her dad.

I round the corner into the main room of the clubhouse and am shocked at the carnage. The floor is littered with broken liquor bottles and booze. There's also blood and bodies, and it's hard to tell what club the deceased belong to.

"Fender!"

I whirl toward the voice and see my father, his shirt soaked in blood, kneeling on the floor. My mother is cocooned in his arms, her body limp. Everything else melts away. The shouting, the gunfire, the mayhem. Cold calm washes over me as I walk toward my parents, ignoring the bullets whizzing past my head. Maybe I'd get lucky, and one would take me out so I wouldn't have to face what I know is coming.

Time speeds up the closer I get. I drop to my knees. "Where are you hit?"

My father's stare is blank, empty. When he doesn't respond, I run my hands over his chest to determine if the blood is his or all from the hole I can now see in my mother's head. I don't allow myself to feel the loss. I can't afford to fall apart right now. My fingers hit a soft spot, a hole, on the left side of my father's chest. I rip the sleeves from his shirt and stuff the fabric in the hole to slow the bleeding. He hisses in pain, but that's his only reaction.

"Stay here," I shout at him, praying he hears what I'm saying. "I'll be back."

I lunge to my feet and storm into the middle of the room. I take a deep breath and find my first target. I point the gun and squeeze the trigger, not stopping until I've systematically taken out every Black Savage still standing, emptying the clip in the process.

"What the fuck was that?" Piston asks, walking through the bodies, kicking a few as he goes.

"Who'd we lose?" I survey the scene, trying to answer my own question.

"Stunner, Carbon, Phantom," Piston rubs his head, leaving a streak of blood. He's looking around, same as me. His head stops moving, and his gaze lands on something behind me. "Aw, fuck."

I slowly turn around, needing to see what he sees, and instantly regret it. My father is slumped over, both my parents dead. It's fitting, I suppose. They lived for the club and died for it. It's what they would've wanted, to go out together in a blaze of glory.

Bang!

I pivot around at the gunshot, shocked to hear it because I thought the chaos was over. Charlie's standing there, her eyes wide, her arms straight, the gun in her hand. I follow her gaze to the man she just killed. Sharp, the Black Savages' Sergeant at Arms, is lying on the floor with a bullet hole between his eyes.

"He was gonna kill you," she mumbles.

"You need to leave," Piston demands. "You don't belong here."

My eyes dart back and forth between the woman I love and my best friend. He's absolutely right. She shouldn't be here. Especially now. But I don't have it in me to make her leave.

"Did you do this?" Joker shouts from behind Piston, directing the question at Charlie. "Precious Black Savages' princess coordinates Soulless Kings' massacre. Isn't spreading your legs enough to secure your place?"

Charlie's arms drop to her sides, and the gun clanks to the floor. She's staring at me, silently begging me to defend her, protect her from the lies my brother's spewing. Problem is, I can't. What if he's right?

"Get the fuck out!" Joker shouts, pointing toward the exit.

Charlie's eyes well with tears as she turns and runs out the front door. In my twenty-three years on this Earth, I've stared down the barrel of a gun more times than I can count, and it doesn't hold a candle to what I'm experiencing right now.

I was born to be a Soulless King, raised to be a ruthless, loyal motherfucker. None of that prepared me for this moment. Nothing could make losing so much any easier to swallow.

They say your life flashes before your eyes at the moment just before death. They fucking lied.

Your life flashes before your eyes at the moment you lose everything you live for.

ALSO BY ANDI RHODES

Broken Rebel Brotherhood

Broken Souls

Broken Innocence

Broken Boundaries

Broken Rebel Brotherhood: Next Generation

Broken Hearts

Broken Wings

Broken Mind

Bastards and Badges

Stark Revenge

Slade's Fall

Jett's Guard

Soulless Kings MC

Fender

Joker

Piston

Greaser

Riker

Trainwreck

Squirrel

Gibson

Flash

Royal

Satan's Legacy MC

Snow's Angel

Toga's Demons

Magic's Torment

Duck's Salvation

Dip's Flame

Devil's Handmaidens MC

Harlow's Gamble

Peppermint's Twist

Mama's Rules

Valhalla Rising MC

Viking

Mayhem Makers

Forever Savage

Saints Purgatory MC

Unholy Soul

Wrathful Malice

Grim's Hell

Shadowy Abyss

Soulless Kings MC: Marble Falls, TX

Crow

ABOUT THE AUTHOR

Andi Rhodes is an author whose passion is creating romance from chaos in all her books! She writes MC (motorcycle club) romance with a generous helping of suspense and doesn't shy away from the more difficult topics. Her books can be triggering for some so consider yourself warned. Andi also ensures each book ends with the couple getting their HEA! Most importantly, Andi is living her real life HEA with her husband and their boxers.

Printed in Great Britain
by Amazon